Blind Secrets

VIBE a Steamy Romance Series 2

Blind Secrets

Lynn Chantale

4 Horsemen
Publications, Inc.

Blind Secrets
VIBE a Steamy Romance Series #2
Copyright © 2021 Lynn Chantale. All rights reserved.

4 Horsemen
Publications, Inc.

4 Horsemen Publications, Inc.
1497 Main St. Suite 169
Dunedin, FL 34698
4horsemenpublications.com
info@4horsemenpublications.com

Cover by 4HP
Typesetting by Michelle Cline
Editor ??

All rights to the work within are reserved to the author and publisher. No part of this publication may be reproduced, stored in a retrieval system, or transmitted in any form or by any means, electronic, mechanical, photocopying, recording, scanning, or otherwise, except as permitted under Section 107 or 108 of the 1976 International Copyright Act, without prior written permission except in brief quotations embodied in critical articles and reviews. Please contact either the Publisher or Author to gain permission.

This is book is meant as a reference guide. All characters, organizations, and events portrayed in this novel are either products of the author's imagination or are used fictitiously. All brands, quotes, and cited work respectfully belongs to the original rights holders and bear no affiliation to the authors or publisher.

Library of Congress Control Number: 2021942115

Print ISBN: 978-1-64450-304-1
Audio ISBN: 978-1-64450-302-7
Ebook ISBN: 978-1-64450-303-4

Table of Contents

Dedication vii
Prologue ix
Chapter One 1
Chapter Two 7
Chapter Three 18
Chapter Four 26
Chapter Five 44
Chapter Six 54
Chapter Seven 68
Chapter Eight 85
Chapter Nine 99
Chapter Ten 106
Chapter Eleven 119
Chapter Twelve 132
Chapter Thirteen 140
Epilogue 146
Author's Note 149

Dedication

To all the wonderful, amazing, and fascinating blind and visually impaired people out there. If you never hear it again, know that you are an inspiration.

Prologue

"This will never work," Victor Grimaldi said.

He stared at the red-haired woman standing at the grave site. Guilt gnawed at his insides as he watched her lower her head. Her hair fell forward, veiling her tears from his scrutiny. *Is this really worth it?* How could he look Amelia in the eye after this? After all, she was his friend.

Victor looked away unable to witness her grief any longer. "She doesn't deserve this," he murmured. "It's not too late to find a better way."

"A better way!" his companion scoffed. "And you deserve to be left alone? Surely, there's a better way to be included in their family." His companion stepped closer, the voice a little more cajoling than before. "Look at them. All sharing in her grief. A family mourning the loss of a respected if despised family member."

Victor shook his head, not wanting to hear the words, yet knowing there was a thread of truth in them. He swallowed hard.

"He's grieving as much as she is, and you can't even comfort him," his companion said with disdain. "Look at them. All the family is there, and where are you?"

Victor once again fastened his gaze on the gravesite and the couple standing there. He could just make out the corner of the American flag peeking from beneath her left arm. Her back was ramrod straight despite her thin shoulders quavering up and down. His heart thudded a little faster when he caught sight of Gage Bedford, a gangly, somewhat awkward youth standing beside the woman.

He towered over her smaller frame. Even at this distance, the youth's stance spoke of comfort and shared sadness. He watched the teen's lips move. She acknowledged the words with a faint nod before he walked away and left her alone again. A faint drizzle misted the air while thunder rumbled in the background.

"At a distance, watching."

The soft words jerked him back to reality. "He doesn't deserve this either," Victor muttered.

"And you do?" the companion demanded. "Quit your whining. She's never gonna know the difference."

Victor swung his gaze back to his companion. "But I know the difference!" He drew a stuttered breath. "She's going to find out." He dragged nervous fingers through his short, cropped hair. Gareth Bedford, a well-built black man and his lover, stepped close to the woman and leaned in. As the man wrapped an arm around her shoulders, a stab of jealousy sliced through his gut. Victor had no right to feel that callous emotion, since he was the source of her pain. Yet...it persisted.

"It's very simple, Victor." The speaker lifted sunglasses and glared through brown eyes. "She's blind; she's grieving. By the time she discovers what happened, things will have progressed too far for her to prevent anything. And if she does find out," Long, thin fingers flicked lint from

Victor's shoulder, a cold smile creasing equally thin lips, making Victor flinch, "I will know exactly who to blame. Understand? She'll marry Gareth Bedford in three or four months, and no one will be the wiser. And no one will know your secret either."

Slowly, Victor nodded. He glanced back at the man and the grieving woman, just as she crumpled to the ground. The man lifted her in his arms and cradled her close. The gangly teen hurried forward. The man shook his head, then nodded toward a line of cars. The youth took off in that direction.

A fresh surge of guilt swamped Victor. There was no way he could keep this from them, but the next words chilled his blood.

"Of course." They watched the couple as well; Gareth was carrying Amelia to a waiting limo. "If she ever learns the truth, before the culmination of my plans, you will know what it's like to grieve for your lover." Returning glasses to face the speaker spun on snazzy heels. "And her death will be on your conscience too."

Three Months Later

The deep, bass line thrummed through the club. Gareth Bedford patted his face with a cotton towel, before he picked up a small bottle of water. Around him, soft moans of delight, whether in pain or pleasure, vied with the resounding smack as a solid implement struck against bare, human flesh.

For a little while, at least, he could forget the grief burdening him the last few months. All around him were the sounds of life, the sounds of adults at play—safe, sane, and consensual kinky activities which stimulated the mind and body in a variety of ways, with a variety of implements: hard, soft and everything in between.

He drew in a steadying breath as he glanced to his left, to where his partner Victor Grimaldi was sprawled in a chair behind a table filled with colorful coils of rope. He was demonstrating a knot to two men. Both appeared to be enthusiasts by the carabiners and safety scissors clipped to the waistbands of their pants.

Gareth hadn't been sure they would participate in the club's annual fetish conference. But one look at the despair in Amelia's eyes, he knew they had to come to the club.

Since becoming a demonstrator at this week-long conference, Gareth had managed to unload most of his inventory of toys; specialty paddles of wood, leather, and Lexan—a form of high impact plastic—were doing brisk sales. Even the rope and leather floggers he typically favored were nearly gone.

Maybe the brisk sales had more to do with his willing submissive and their obvious enjoyment of the implements he employed on their willing flesh.

Gareth slid a practiced finger along the darkening welt between Amelia's shoulder blades. She stilled at his touch before she continued to wiggle and squirm in the ropes at her wrists.

He chanced a glance at the crowd. It was a good size, maybe about twenty or thirty spectators—most in some state of undress or fetish wear. He admired the couple in the back. The man wore a mask which hid his entire face, a studded leather collar with the word Pet outlined in crystals attached to a short leash. The man's torso was bare. The woman holding the leash wore a bad wig and a jeweled half mask. There was something about the set of her mouth he recognized but couldn't place.

Movement caught his peripheral. Amelia was working the knots at her wrists. She was still secured to the I-ring on the overhead suspension rig for that purpose. But she would get free from the rope tethering her to the bolt. He bit back a smile. She never failed to amaze him at her skill of undoing the secured knots.

Even better was seeing her smiling. It assured him he'd made the right decision. Joshua's death hit them all hard, but it devastated Amelia. She was thinner. Her frame had always been trim and toned, but the recent weight loss gave her an almost gaunt appearance. He didn't like that. In fact, he was more concerned than he let on. It almost seemed like she was trying to die. But he would never allow that. Not when she still had so much life left to live. Besides, he promised Joshua, if anything should happen to him, that he would take care of Amelia.

So here they were in an exclusive dungeon and sex club for the week. The adjacent hotel provided conference goers with overnight accommodations.

He scanned the large room. Most of the time, this room held a bevy of pool tables and several free-standing suspension rigs. The rigs were in place, but a few of the pool tables had been moved away to make room for demonstrations.

Those who had chosen to follow along as he'd rigged the harness around Amelia were just about finished. From the work displayed, many had a working knowledge of tying, and a few he knew were into shibari—an ancient, artistic form of Japanese rope bondage.

He smiled as he dragged a simple caress down his partner's bare arm. She trembled beneath his touch. He briefly admired his handiwork. Ropes of red and purple crisscrossed her torso in a pentagram, then to the harness cinched at her waist, to her thighs and calves.

"I specialize in comfortable suspension for all sizes," Gareth explained. "And if you have a sub who likes to wiggle out of her bonds..."

As if on cue, Amelia lifted her arms, trailing the ends of her ropes. The small cluster of people in the room let out a chorus of laughter.

"Who is prone to escaping?" Amelia challenged.

In one hand, he picked up the trailing end of the rope, then grabbed her with the other. She laughed as he pressed her against him. "You are such a brat, Amelia," he murmured into her ear.

⇝

Amelia Bedford grinned. "Yes, I am," she said. It was the first real moment of freedom she'd experienced in months. Nothing could detract her from the heady rush of excitement coursing through her veins. After the funeral, so many of the details still hazy, she had begged for death's oblivion. The closest she got to that was sleep and that was tormented by dreams of him. Her Joshua.

As if sensing her thoughts, Gareth plunged his fingers through her hair, then caressing her throat with the rope. The soft hemp fluttered over the sensitive skin, and she sighed.

"Rope isn't just something to bind your partner. It's also a seduction." He trailed his fingers, then the rope, down her throat, to her breasts, to the apex of her thighs and back again. He walked behind her, his fingers never leaving her body as he reach for a carabiner with his free hand. "And while you employ a bit of seduction," he clipped the loop to the harness, "you can secure your sub in place."

A smattering of laughter and applause filled her ears. "You don't play fair," she said with a giggle.

"Stay in the now with me," he said to her, for her ears alone. "Since my sub and I are very familiar with one another, you'll notice I did not use as much rope as we've done in earlier demonstrations." He slowly pulled on the rope, taking up the slack, then tying it off with a square knot, Carefully, he pulled on the rope until Amelia's feet left the floor.

Briefly, she sat back in a weightless disorientation until Gareth touched her shoulder.

"Breathe," he whispered.

She did as he commanded, her body adjusting, then welcoming the soft bite of rope as her arms and legs slowly extended until she resembled a starfish. She was open, vulnerable and exposed.

And she felt alive!

Gareth's words faded until all that remained was the gentle cadence of his deep basso, his touch, and the gentle swing of the rope. She was lifted and lowered. Her limbs positioned at will. She was swung slow, fast, and everything in between.

This was what she needed. Her mind blanked until all that remained was the sensation of exquisite pain and floating. Peace soothed overwrought nerves and emotions.

She longed to stay like this forever. The faint scent of cinnamon and apples enveloped her.

She sighed. "Gareth."

His fingers were gentle as he touched her fingers and toes. "A few more minutes, love."

"As you can see, she's quite docile now, well into subspace, or that trance-like state where euphoria is her best friend." He kept his voice low and soothing.

"What were you just doing?" a male voice from the back demanded.

"Could you be a little more specific? I've been doing a lot."

"You seemed to be pinching her toes and such."

"Oh. Checking the circulation. When she's this relaxed, it's very important to make sure circulation is maintained. And since we've been spinning," he gave the rope a little shake; Amelia did not move, "it's important to check often that the lines don't tangle and become too tight."

He patted his shirt pocket, then his waistband. "Call me overprotective, but I typically carry two pairs of safety scissors on my person at all times, while Amelia carries a pair in her bra strap when she's self-tying."

"Will we get to see any of her self-tying tonight?" the man demanded.

Gareth smiled. "Not tonight. We've gone over our time already." He moved back to Amelia, held her body close as he grabbed the mainline to release the tension. Slowly, he lowered her to the floor, promptly covering her with a light blanket as he knelt beside her. "It's also important to give your sub time to calm down from your play. Don't be alarmed when you see grooves left in skin after removing the ropes. Depending on how tight and how long the suspension, the marks will disappear in a few days."

Victor set a bottle of water at Gareth's elbow. "Thanks, love." He nodded, then returned to his seat behind the table.

Voices murmured and buzzed around Amelia. She was aware of her breathing, slow and deep. Counting each heartbeat, she settled more into herself. The smooth silk sheet beneath her cheek eased her back to reality. The slight weight of the fuzzy blanket also added comfort and warmth. Now she could focus on the wonderful burn of the rope enveloping her limbs. She traced the braided cotton, her fingers finding the grooves from earlier times. A satisfied smile creased her lips. The marks would be slow to leave her body and that was just how she wanted it.

When she stirred, gentle hands lowered one corner of her blanket from her face. Cool air kissed her cheeks, and a straw tapped her lips. She drank.

"So how long does she stay on the floor?"

"As long as she wants," Gareth replied, a faint edge in his voice.

The scent of something sickly sweet and perfumy filled her nostrils. Then, a cold hand seized her ankle, and she gasped. Just like that, she was jerked back into the reality as vibrations from the surrounding music pulsed through the floor and into her. There was no going back to that sweet spot of good feelings.

"Don't touch her!" Menace filled the deep basso. "You always ask permission before touching someone else's toy. Living or not."

"I was just trying to get a better look at the marks," a male spectator said.

Tension filled the silence, enough to make Amelia lift her head. Her mind was fully alert now despite her body wanting to stay put.

The male spectator let out an annoyed huff.

Gareth smoothed her hair from her face. "You're okay, love. Just lie there as long as you need." To the man, he said, "You need to back off and give us some space."

"I don't see what the big deal is," the man muttered.

"And unfortunately, I don't have time to teach you," Gareth snapped. "Two-Z, please give our friend a crash course in Etiquette 101."

Once Two-Z, a lithe mocha skinned woman in a curve-hugging leather bustier and stilettos, firmly pulled the offender off to the side, Gareth began untying Amelia's ropes. As he tossed the ropes aside, Victor picked them up and coiled them into a canvas bag on the table.

Gareth massaged her arms and wrist before moving to her thighs and ankles.

Satisfied that she was not injured, he helped her sit, then placed the blanket around her shoulders once more.

"We pushed that a little far," Gareth told her.

She leaned her head against his shoulder. "I needed the release."

"I know." He pushed a bottle of water into her hands. "Hydrate."

Voices moved around her as she drank. Once she finished that bottle, another was placed into her hands.

"We'll grab a bite after the room clears a bit," Gareth assured her.

She sipped her water more slowly. "I don't think I can eat anything."

"You'll eat something." His tone was firm. "You've lost too much weight since—" He stopped. "Since the funeral. You know he'd come back and kill me if I didn't take care of you."

Tears burned behind her lids. "I just miss him so much." She fingered the triangular locket at her throat. "I don't want this moment to end."

"I miss him too, Amelia."

"I want to do some self-tying later."

"Only if you eat something," he countered.

She giggled. "Okay."

They sat a moment longer, not as many voices in the vicinity and she frowned.

"What's wrong?" Gareth prompted.

"You're not putting away the ropes."

"No, Victor took care of it for me."

She sensed rather than heard the hesitancy. "What happened?"

"The guy I asked Two-Z to talk with, I don't like the way he's been watching you."

"Is he the one who touched me?"

"Yes."

"His hands were cold. I didn't like his vibe, and I'm very glad you covered me with the blanket."

"Most of the people here we know. There are only a handful I've never met, and he's one of them."

"I think I'm ready."

Gareth helped her to her feet, then pulled a silk chemise over her head. She placed her arms through the straps, and Gareth adjusted them on her shoulders while the rest of the garment skimmed her curves and stopped mid-thigh.

He adjusted the bodice. "For a woman, you are pretty damn sexy!"

She chuckled. "Coming from you, that's high praise indeed."

He skimmed a finger over the curve of her cheek. "You're smiling again. He would like that."

A single tear escaped. She inhaled a stuttered breath. "I miss him so much," she admitted. "Some days...it's so bad my bones ache from missing him."

Gareth rested his forehead on hers and placed his hand on her hips. "After you get something to eat, we'll walk a bit, then grab your private room so you can self-tie."

She closed her eyes against the flood of tears.

Gareth nodded to Victor as Amelia slipped into a pair of jeweled flip-flops. The room was now empty. Two club employees walked in with spray bottles and a vacuum cleaner. The room would be wiped down and cleaned before the next demonstration later that night. "Thank you."

"Hey. You two looked great. What was up with that wanker touching AM?" Victor shouldered the canvas bag.

Gareth swung an arm around Victor's shoulders "He was just a tad excited."

The trio walked from the room into the dim lighting of a wide corridor.

Music pulsed while laughter and moans punctuated the bass line. People in various garb or women wearing with only pasties or the equivalent of the two roamed back and forth between the rooms.

As they passed one room, Gareth caught a glimpse of a leather-clad woman wielding a cat-o'-nine-tails whip. Her subject, a naked flabby older man, writhed with each strike. The watching crowd oohed and ached with each hard strike. "Please tell me you two have decided to eat; I'm famished."

Amelia snorted. "When aren't you famished?" she teased. Victor poked her in the ribs. She squealed and wiggled away. "Stop! You know I'm ticklish."

"And wasting away on me." He grabbed her hand. "C'mon, love, the hotel restaurant next door has a positively decadent chocolate cake that is sinful just to even inhale."

"Chocolate?" she perked up. "There's always room for chocolate."

Over Amelia's head, Gareth mouthed, "Thank you."

Victor nodded. "And if you have room after cake, they have pulled pork sliders." Gareth followed their progress up the hall toward the elevator alcove.

Two-Z fell in step with him. "A word?"

"Victor." Gareth waited until the other man turned his head. "Order for me."

Victor nodded, then disappeared around the corner.

"What's up?"

"Keep an eye on that guy," Two-Z warned. "There's something really off about him."

Gareth ran a hand over his scalp. "Did he say something?"

"Just a feeling. He's extremely interested in AM. Enough that I wouldn't leave her unattended."

He nodded in understanding. "We'll be around for a couple of more hours. She needs to do some self-tying and once done, I'll take her home."

Two-Z placed a hand on his arm. "I'm glad you got her to come tonight. We've all been grieving for and with her. Sir J was a very good man." She stepped back. "If she ever needs me in a top capacity or just as a friend, let me know, and I'm there."

Gareth leaned down and kissed her cheek. Thanks, I'll let her know."

"Tell her I have a new flogger she'll like."

He walked away, her laughter following him around the corner.

Amelia sat on the floor. The light was so low in the room, it almost felt nonexistent. This was her time. Gareth and Victor would be her spotters, but this was her time. She wiggled her toes, then reached a hand to the several bundles of rope at her side. She started with her ankles The stupid buckle knot took her six months to get right. A faint smile touched her lips. She moved to her thighs, working quickly but efficient through each knot and twist to complete her harness. She stood, winding a length of rope around her hips, giving herself enough to complete the rig she needed.

She held up a hand, reaching for the carabiner on the suspension rack. When it met her fingers, she looped the rope from it through her waist harness.

"Double check the door," Gareth told Victor. "I'll start the music."

A soft click reached her ears, even as the opening strains of a Sam Smith song filled the room. The tune was slow, wistful, and hit just the right level of love angst.

She sighed, then slowly sat back.

"Hold on, love, you forgot your scissors." Gareth knelt before her and fastened the shears to her bra strap.

"Thanks. Now go away."

He chuckled, and she listened to his footsteps fade. His clothing rustled as he sat somewhere near her right.

She swayed, getting a feel for the rope. She raised one leg, then tied off. She sat back, lifting her body until she was nearly a foot off the floor, allowing her thoughts to fade away. Victor and Gareth murmured to one another, but it wasn't intrusive. In fact, it was comforting. The slow music, and the subtle scent of lavender and sage, coupled with the free spin, settled her as nothing else had.

She raised and lowered her body, spinning in dizzying circles, then moving to slow spirals.

"I need some water," she muttered.

"Sure," said Gareth

Amelia wasn't sure, but it sounded as if Gareth slurred the word. The water was cool and refreshing as it splashed over her tongue. He raised the bottle again, and she shook her head.

"Thanks." She wanted to spin a little longer. A soft thud met her ears, but she dismissed it as the water bottle fell to the floor.

"I'll be right back. I gotta visit the loo." Victor shuffled from the room.

She caught a breeze as Victor passed, leaving a faint scent of spiced rot trailing behind him. The odd odor briefly caught her off guard, and her hand slipped from the brake.

She dropped a few inches but quickly regained her hold. Once more, she settled into her float and spun, but her stomach wouldn't settle. Several times, she lost her grip and nearly fell. "Gareth? Something's wrong. Gareth?"

"N..."

Thud. Click!

Her heart pinned a little louder. "Gareth? Victor? Something's wrong with Gareth."

Cold hands closed over hers. "Everything is just right."

The scent of spiced decay enveloped her, and she gagged. Before she realized what he was doing, her hands were tied, and she was left to hang upside down.

"Stop," she pleaded. Even to her ears, her words were feeble and slurred.

"I've been wanting to do this for a long, long time."

At the crack of a single tail whip, she flinched. The first strike dried the saliva in her mouth. After the second, she didn't remember screaming.

Chapter One

Three Years Later

Laughter floated in the room. Conversations buzzed in small pockets as quiet music mingled with the 'festivities. Amelia shifted in her chair, adjusting the strap of the leash beneath her thigh. Her guide dog, Kiska laying at her feet.

"There must be accountability amongst the sighted community," a male voice raised above everything else. "There is no excuse for the way they treat us."

"I swear...he gets louder with every meeting we have," Penelope muttered. "If I could actually see him, I'd squirt him with a water gun."

Amelia smothered a chuckle. "For someone so obnoxious, he does manage to make a difference in the blind community."

"That's his only saving grace," Penelope said. "Thank goodness the meeting is over, and all we're waiting on is our checks."

Amelia nodded, even though she knew her friend wouldn't see the movement. She enjoyed the meetings because their organization did a lot of good, advocating and helping others who are blind or visually impaired. But there were days she wished Murphy Giles would keep his mouth shut.

The monthly meeting was also a chance for them to socialize over a meal while they conducted business, and the restaurant served fantastic food and strong drinks. Another added bonus, the servers all knew their group and were quick to help without being condescending.

This group made Amelia feel normal. If she bumped into someone, no explanation was needed. The majority of the individuals in the room knew the challenges and triumphs of navigating a sighted world with little to no vision at all. Amelia had very limited vision, only seeing certain colors and vague shapes, but that never stop her from living a full, productive life.

Even knowing one of her firm associates had tried to falsify information on a trust she facilitated couldn't detract from the occasion. Not only had she found the discrepancy, but she terminated the lawyer immediately. Frowning, she shook her head. Not quite understanding why Peter Tyler, with his brilliant mind and promising career, would throw everything away. At the very least, disbarment, the maximum sentence—prison.

Amelia didn't care to prosecute; she just wanted him gone from the firm. By discovering Chad's betrayal, she'd saved her firm several million in fines and reparations. Even more so, their reputation and her name.

Which was all she had left of him—Joshua.

She touched the triangular locket nestled in the hollow of her throat. The pain wasn't as sharp as before, but the burn was still there, reminding her the dull ache of love would never ease, would never be the same without him, without Joshua.

She pushed away the melancholy.

The firm was intact. No one, but the partners, knew of the indiscretion, and it would stay that way. She drained the rest of her long island iced tea. Now that all was well, she could take a much-needed leave. Oh, she would still be around for a few select clients, but for the most part, she wouldn't have to step into the law firm of Hastings, Bedford, and Associates if she could help it. Her specialty was in Trust and Estate Law. The Bedford was in reference to Gareth Bedford. He'd assumed his father's role in the partnership and thrived on corporate and intellectual property rights. And because oath at association, the firm somehow had been drafted into commercial contracts for some of the State's largest companies.

Footsteps sounded on the thing carpet before a hand gripped the back of her chair. Amelia tensed as an arm brushed her shoulder.

"Here ya go, hon," the server said. "I've placed your check next to your left hand."

Amelia blew out a breath as the woman moved away. "Thank you." She reached for the small plastic tray, then fumbled in her wallet for money.

"Did you hear about Mr. VIP?" A snatch of conversation filled the silence.

Amelia paused, her fingers grazing the bills in her wallet. Mr. VIP was one of her firm's clients. She didn't handle his issue personally, but she was privy to the details, and it saddened her.

Vector Integrated Practices had been around for a long time and knowing the circumstances of why the company had to dissolve was just disgusting. Not even re-organization could salvage what was left of the small, once powerful, tech company.

What she would miss most about Mr. VIP was his understanding of what those with visual impairments needed in computer software. He had a knack for getting existing software to work better with the new programs he had developed.

Even she used one of his programs which helped her keep track of motions, briefs, and obscure legal references.

"I heard his wife left him for another man." This voice was brash and held a masculine quality but wasn't a man. "And he gambled away company funds."

"Oh, Ana, don't start gossiping," someone else admonished.

"Why can't people mind their own business?" Penelope demanded, annoyance flaring in her voice. "If the man wanted everybody to know his business, he'd have announced it himself."

"They're only talking about him 'cause he's not here," Amelia replied. "I'm going to take Kiska out before my ride gets here." She placed bills on the tray, then pushed it toward what she hoped was the center of the table. She was also hoping to distract from the conversation still buzzing in the room.

"No limos tonight?" Penelope teased.

"Not tonight." She chuckled. "Thought I'd try Uber for a change." Amelia stood, holding the leash. Kiska came alert with a jangle of tags and a vigorous shake. "C'mon, girl, let's find the door out."

Taking a loose grip on the harness handle, Amelia allowed the dog to guide her from the room. She kept pace with the dog's quick, sure steps. Patrons oohed and aahed as they wove their way through the restaurant.

"I have the door for you," a friendly voice called.

"Thanks." Amelia smiled as the cool night air kissed her face.

She heaved a sigh once they made it into the relative quiet of the sidewalk. Wavering slightly, to catch her bearings, she grimaced. Maybe she shouldn't have downed that last bit of alcohol. Still, she enjoyed the slight buzz.

If memory served her right, there was a patch of grass about twenty yards to her left. "Left," she prompted the dog. At once, the animal did as commanded. After a few paces, they stopped. Amelia felt forward with her foot and discovered they were at a curb. "Good girl. Forward, I have it now."

They crossed the expanse of asphalt without incident. Small pebbles crunched beneath her shoes before they were muffled by grass. She stopped, then removed the harness by pushing in the hinge clip. She pulled the apparatus off and looped it over her shoulder. She readied a poop bag just in case and gave the command, "busy, busy," for the dog to relieve herself.

"All right, girl." Amelia followed a few steps as Kiska sniffed and turned. A moment later, a soft hiss filled the night. Amelia shoved the unused bag in her pocket, then re-harnessed the dog. "All right, girl, let's go back."

Tires screeched in the distance. Amelia walked until her shoes touched the edge of grass and the beginning of asphalt. She listened for a moment. *Still no traffic on this edge of the parking lot.*

"Find the curb," Amelia said. Kiska moved and Amelia stepped forward.

An engine raced. Someone screamed a warning as Kiska stopped, then dragged her backward.

Amelia lost her balance, trying to compensate for the sudden change in direction. Air sped past her, and something clipped her hip, aiding her fall. She hit the ground hard, sprawled into a heap.

Kiska danced next to her, nudging her face, emitting a soft whine.

Footsteps pounded on the pavement. She reached a shaky hand to calm her dog.

"It's okay, girl. You did good. You saved my life." She hugged the dog and allowed the animal to lick her face.

"Are you alright?" Voices moved around her. "That car tried to run you over."

Chapter Two

Victor sat across from a handsome young man with unruly dark hair, studying the other male beneath his lashes. Simple but the boy was beautiful. Dark curly hair, chiseled cheekbones, deep-set brown eyes that seemed to hold a perpetual gleam of mischief, and wide mouth already bracketed with laugh lines.

And wondered, not for the first time, if the young man was his son.

"If you keep this up, I'll have your king in three moves," the younger man said with mirth. "Where is your head today?"

"Not on the game," Victor admitted. With effort, he refocused on the chess board. Indeed, if he didn't pay more attention, Gage's bishop would take his king. "You leave me no bloody good choices."

Now, Gage laughed. "Shoulda been paying attention rather than fantasizing about your date last night."

If only... Victor thought. All these years and the closest he'd gotten to his love was a cottage on the edge of the estate. He studied Gage from beneath his lashes. They had the same dark hair and brown eyes, but that was all they shared. If he could know for certain, he could get out of the trouble he was in.

Maybe. But knowing with certainty that Gage was the product of a long ago menage a trois could possibly create more issues, especially with his lover, Gareth. There was no way Gareth could forgive or understand. Even if the tryst occurred before he had fallen for Gareth.

His gaze wandered the length of the family room. It was as wide as it was long. Despite this, the warm pecan paneling, the soft peach paint, and the fun accent pillows in shades of greens, blues, and golds gave the space a cozy, lived-in feel. He and Gage sat in a grouping of chairs near the built-in shelves currently holding a bevy of board games. To his left was the entrance to the house and a granite-topped bar. Padded stools sat beneath it, facing the 80-inch flat screen on the wall behind. To his right, slightly behind, was another grouping—this one centered around an elaborate stone fireplace. A colorful woven rug sat in front of the hearth.

In front of him were French doors leading to a screened terrace where he could just make out a large, bald, black man pacing back and forth.

His heart skipped a beat as his muscles flexed and rippled beneath his cotton shirt. A phone was pressed to his ear. Just who was Gareth yelling at?

"Do not take that tone of voice with me!" a strident voice warned. "No! It's your job to know where every dime goes."

Victor held his breath as his heart pounded in his chest. "Did Gareth know what he'd done?

"No. I'm done with your excuses," Gareth continued.

"Sounds like big bro is pissing in somebody's corn flakes," Gage said with a grin. "I love hearing him rip someone a new one." He studied the board for all of three seconds, picked up his knight, then smacked the black queen from the board. "Checkmate."

"Bugger it!"

Gage laughed. "Your head ain't in this at all."

"Of course I hired someone else! You're lucky I don't have you arrested. As it is, if you return what's mine, my attorney won't go after your license," Gareth promised.

Victor's cell rang. He fumbled the device from his pocket, nearly dropping it on the parquet floor. "What?"

"What's all the yelling about?" Leigh Olsen entered, swinging a Kate Spade bag by the shoulder strap. Dawson Cahill, Bedford social secretary and pseudo-butler, hurried in after.

"I'm sorry Mr. Bedford. She insisted on coming in," the man apologized, practically breathless.

Gage caught the slight sneer before Dawson blanked his features. "Don't worry about it."

"The yelling?" Leigh insisted.

If Gage hadn't been watching, he'd have missed the look passing from Dawson to Leigh.

Victor paled. *Curious.*

Gage shrugged as Victor stood and crossed the room. He stopped at the far end near the fireplace and kept his back to them. "Seems like someone's stealing from Gar, and Victor is pissy 'cause I schooled him in chess," Gage said.

"I want a rematch," Victor said, covering the mouthpiece.

"When you can pay attention to the game," Gage retorted.

Leigh dropped her handbag in a club chair and made straight for the cart full of liquor in the corner. "Don't you ever do anything less boring?" She waved a manicured hand. "Chess and money."

"Perhaps strategy eludes your more simplistic endeavors of shopping and massages."

Leigh tossed back her perfectly coiffed, chestnut hair. Gage studied her a moment. She could've been pretty if she didn't have the personality of a wolf spider. Some creepy-crawly vibe leaked from her dark brown eyes. It didn't help that she was long and thin, furthering the impression of an arachnid. Gage wondered what web she was spinning now and who she planned to trap in it.

She stared at him. "Was that some sort of insult?"

"The fact that you have to ask ...never mind." Gage put away the chess pieces.

Gareth strode into the room, stopping short when he saw Leigh. "You are trespassing."

"I came to see Amelia." She managed a pout. "She refuses to see me." She raised the glass of scotch to her lips. "I worry about her."

"Right. Why are you really here?" A colder edge crept into his voice.

"She's my sister."

"Half-sister," Gareth pointed out. "As you're so fond of reminding her and anyone else who is dumb enough to listen."

Leigh set her tumbler down with a snap. She snatched up her purse, then slapped down a thick envelope on the counter. "You are just a horrid man."

"Nice of you to notice." Gareth looked at Gage. "Where's Victor?"

Gage nodded toward the far end of the room.

"Make sure she doesn't walk out with the silver," Gareth warned.

Gage stood, holding the boxed chess game. He flashed a wolfish smile. "I guess that means you should keep your hands where I can see them at all times."

She huffed. "You're just as horrid as your brother."

"I don't much like you either." Gage set the box on a nearby shelf. "So which dying millionaire are you banging this week?" He was pleased to see the rush of color on her artfully made-up face. The natural color rivaled the faint blush she wore.

"Don't be so gauche." She dropped her purse onto the counter. "Tell Amelia I stopped by to give her some papers from her grandmother. The lawyer dropped them off."

Gage crossed the room to where the envelope lay. "So why didn't the lawyer bring them here? Amelia's lived here for almost three years now."

Saying nothing, Leigh strolled out, high heels clicking on the polished wood floor, the door slamming in the distance announced her departure.

"What do you think you're doing?" Gareth demanded.

Victor shook his head. "Leave it alone, Gare. This has nothing to do with you."

"The hell it does!" He looked around, grabbed Victor by the elbow, then pulled him onto the terrace, away from prying ears. Humid air greeted them while the scent of lilacs, roses and fresh mulch permeated the space. The motion activated fans swirled a cool breeze. "This does concern me. What kind of trouble are you in?"

Victor studied the other man. Concern, confusion, love were written in every line of his handsome face. Again, Victor shook his head. "It's better if you don't know."

Wordlessly, Gareth pulled a sheet of papers from his pocket, then handed them to Victor. "You mean more to me than anything else in this world. All you had to do was come to me."

Victor crumpled the papers in his fist. The evidence of his betrayal written in black and white. "Is that why you married her?"

"You convinced me to marry her!" Gareth closed his eyes, then stared into Victor's. "She is the reason we are even living in the same house without the scrutiny of our relatives. She's why you can stand there and accuse me of not loving you, and better yet, she's the reason why you're stealing from her."

He flinched, as if struck. "I'm not..." He lowered his voice. "I'm not stealing from anybody."

Gareth folded his arms across his massive chest.

"Look. I know what it looks like, but it's not what it is." He ran agitated fingers through his hair. "Look, Gare, just leave it alone."

"I can't. Just like I've promised to love and protect you, I've promised her the same thing. You know what her family is like. Do you know what they've done to her?"

Victor's heart skipped a beat. Of course he knew. He was complicit in dealing Amelia the ultimate emotional blow. And in doing so, he mucked up things for himself as well. "Gareth, you're sticking your nose where it doesn't belong."

Gareth merely raised an eyebrow.

"Don't look at me like that." Victor shoved the papers back at Gareth. "Forget you saw this. I don't want to lose you."

Gareth caught him by the wrist. "What do you mean lose me?"

Victor shook him off. "Just leave it alone. You both have more money than any one person can spend in a lifetime. Let alone ten. What's a few thousand every now and then?"

"Victor, what's wrong?"

How did he tell this man he was in way over his head? That somehow, what started as a simple revenge had gotten way out of pocket? That some secrets were better left buried. That he only did this now to keep Gareth alive.

"This isn't you, Victor. You've lost weight, and you're drinking more. Something is going on with you."

Victor cupped Gareth's face. "Know that I love you more than my next breath. The only way to keep you safe is to continue what I'm doing. Please don't ask me to do anything else." With that, he walked away.

Gareth briefly stared after him before retrieving the fallen papers. He stuffed them into his pocket as he walked back into the house. He noted Dawson halfway between the liquor cart and the door. The butler froze. "We will have words later, Dawson." Gareth held the servant's gaze, noting a flicker of fear? "That is the last time you let an undesirable in my home."

"But sir—"

"You are employed by me, not my parents!" he stated. The quietness of his voice cut every bit as deep as if he'd yelled. "You are on notice."

Dawson collected the dirty glass, the tumbler rattling against the tray as he left the room.

Heels clicked across the tile. Gareth whirled and found Leigh strolling in, as if she owned the place. "I forgot my purse."

"Rather convenient," Gage muttered under his breath.

Gareth breathed deep, regaining his composure. "What did that little viper want?" He stared right into Leigh's dark brown eyes as he spoke. While Leigh and Amelia had the same pale, mocha skin, indicative of biracial parents, that's where the similarities ended.

Leigh's dark, wavy locks framed her narrow face in an attempt to distract from her high forehead. Dark brown mascara and eyeliner ringed her beady eyes. And for the first time, Gareth thought her gaze reminded him of an insect. Even her body, though clothed in designer clothes, gave the same impression—short, thin torso with long skinny limbs.

"She says the lawyer dropped off some papers from Amelia's grandmother." Gage held up the envelope.

Gareth covered the distance in three long strides and plucked the envelope from his brother's outstretched fingers. He inspected the paper. "This has been opened."

Leigh managed a bitter laugh. "Of course it has. I had to see what that old bat had to say. Amelia wasn't even her blood relative."

Gareth stepped forward, menace in every stride. Eyes widening, Leigh stumbled back. "Haven't you people done enough to her?" he demanded. "It's not enough that you ridicule and demean her at every chance, but now...you want to steal her inheritance as well?"

Some of the color and smugness drained from her face. She held up a hand, as if warding off the statement. "She only got what she did because..."

"Because she genuinely loved her grandmother," he snapped. "Unlike the rest of you who constantly have your hand out and eyes firmly closed to her plight. Hester Lee was a woman of sound mind, and she knew exactly what her grandchildren wanted from her. Maybe that's why she left Amelia what she did, to the one person who saw her as a human being and not some money bag."

Leigh clutched her purse until her knuckles paled. "I see you are distraught."

"Distraught doesn't even cover what I am right now." Gareth tossed the envelope onto the table. "I will make sure to go over the papers with Amelia. From now on, there will be no more of her signing what you give her unless I facilitate it."

Gareth closed the distance between them, using his height and mass to intimidate the much smaller woman. He lowered his voice so only she would hear. "I know exactly what you've done. Once I have proof, you and the rest of your ilk are going down." He stepped away.

Now Leigh did look sick. She stumbled from the room.

"Now who's the one in distress," Gage murmured. "Dang, big bro, if you put a little more bass into your voice, you could've gotten her to pee herself."

Despite the lingering tension, Gareth smiled. "Do you ever take anything serious?"

Gage nodded. "Food, music, chess, and sex. But not necessarily in that order." He studied his brother a moment. "Is someone trying to hurt Amelia?"

He ran a hand over his scalp. "I honestly don't know," he confessed. "You heard about the car?"

Gage nodded.

"Some say it was deliberate" Gareth said. "Others say it was just an accident. Either way, I'm wary."

"But she's okay, right?"

"She's as fine as can be"

"Did you really mean her family is stealing from her?"

Gareth nodded.

"That's just…"

Gareth picked up the envelope and pulled out the papers. He scanned the pages. "Well isn't this interesting," he mused, grinning. "It seems we may have another mole at the office." He folded the papers carefully, replacing them in the envelope. "Amelia knows exactly what's going on. For weeks now, she has the real files in braille and audio."

"I can't believe it took two and a half years to settle her estate."

"With so much at stake, Hester Lee knew what she was doing."

Victor rushed in, face pale. "I need to talk to you."

"Now you want to talk?"

Gage stood. "Well, on that note, I'll see if Amelia wants chocolate cake before I practice my tuba."

Victor waited until Gage was well out of earshot before he said, "I need you to trust me."

Gareth studied him. A hint of panic flashed in Victor's water blue eyes. The emotion tugged at his heart. What could've transpired in the last few minutes to give this man before him a sense of desperation? "What makes you think I don't?"

Relief washed over Victor. "Can we just leave for the weekend without you asking questions?"

He searched his memory for anything that could've sent Victor into this spiral, but only one thing fit. Gareth perused the pages. "I'm presuming this will be like any other weekend where we run off together."

Victor hesitated.

"You know, the only way any of this works is if she's there," he gently pointed out.

Victor flinched as if struck.

Gareth hated seeing distress on his lover's face, but his hands were tied. If he was going to protect his loved ones, he had to do this. No matter how much it hurt them both.

"Fine. Whatever." Victor said, disappointment and resentment oozing from every syllable.

"Do you think this is easy for me?" Gareth demanded, holding Victor's gaze. "Pretending to be straight when I'm not. To keep how I feel about you from my family and deny your rightful place as my spouse."

Victor gripped Gareth's hands into his, hope shining on his handsome face. "Then just do it. Forget about your family. Divorce Amelia and let's be together."

"Because it's not about me or you. If I don't run the family business, there's nothing for Gage."

"One of these days, your bloody nobility will get you killed."

"And so will your selfishness."

Chapter Three

Amelia basked in the sunlight, relishing the warmth on her skin. She lazily drifted her fingers through the silky fur of her guide dog, Kiska. When she lifted her hand, the dog's cold nose bumped it. She laughed. "You are so demanding," she said. "But you keep me safe."

Lazing in the sun was a nice way to unwind from the rigors of her career, allowing her aching hip time to heal. Had it only been a few days since her mishap with the car? She hugged Kiska, grateful for her well-trained guide.

The sultry alto of Toni Braxton faded into the DJ's melodious tones. The warm voice was serious as it gave the latest news. "Police are asking anyone with information to please call. This is a real blow to the community. Our hearts and prayers go out to the family of Teena Williams, owner of Tranquility Helping Hands. She was found brutally murdered."

Amelia tuned out the rest of what the DJ said. She'd recommended the company to clients until she learned the owner was incapable of managing her profits wisely. Too bad the woman was dead; she actually had a good business despite so many small businesses falling away. She'd have to speak to Gareth. Maybe there was something he could do.

A bell pealed near her elbow. She fumbled for the device velcroed to the chair's arm. "Yes."

"It's me, Amelia," Gage announced. "Would you like to split a piece of cake with me?"

Amelia smiled at the melodious voice. Between her brother-in-law and Gareth, they were the only ones to keep her sane after... She pushed the square button outlined in felt. "There better be a glass of milk with that cake," she called.

"Please tell me you're decent. I don't want to see my brother's wife naked."

She laughed. "Swimsuit and coverup."

Shoes scraped on cement, and a moment later, a clink of china on metal filled her ears, followed by the creak of the chair beside her. "The plate is right next to your left hand and the spoon is on the plate," Gage said. "Our beverages of choice are chilling in the ice bucket."

"Gareth always teases me when he sees a bottle of milk chilling like a fine champagne."

"He doesn't know what he's missing."

"What made you decide to come visit?"

"Things were getting a little tense downstairs."

"Victor and Gareth arguing again?"

"I don't think what they do is actually called arguing. It's more like two CEO's trying to prove who's the manliest."

She snorted. "Apt description."

"No one was happy to see Leigh."

"Dawson let her into the house again," she stated rather than asked.

Amelia couldn't imagine what Leigh wanted when Leigh knew she wasn't welcomed in the house. Amelia frowned. *What game is Leigh playing this time?*

"Gare was not pleased. He put him on notice."

She suppressed a shudder. "Good. I don't like that man. And I don't like how he keeps letting Leigh in."

"Me either." Silverware clinked on china. "You wanna listen to me practice my tuba when we're done here?"

"You don't even have to ask." Amelia settled her plate in her lap, keeping one finger near the moist cake as she used the spoon to scoop a helping into her mouth. As the creamy, rich goodness melted on her tongue, she sighed in utter satisfaction. She truly needed this. "Now that is how you enjoy chocolate cake."

They sat in companionable silence. Only the clink of silverware on china filled the space. An occasional bird called, mingling with the crickets and cicadas, and the mellow R&B flowing from the radio.

A warm breeze brought the scent of fetid sweat and stale masculinity so potent and familiar, an overwhelming wave of panic swamped her. She couldn't swallow the morsels of cake lodged in her throat. The spoon dropped from her fingers with a clatter.

He is back. She had to run, but she was rooted to the spot.

"Hey, do you smell that?" Gage asked.

Blood roared in her ears, drowning out everything but her own frantic heartbeats. "Pickles," she murmured. She swung her legs from the chaise, forgetting she still had the plate of cake. The china hit the floor, scattering glass and crumbs over her bare feet. Breath congealed in her chest, refusing the stingiest sip of air while her mind flitted in a kaleidoscope of chaos. *How did he find me?*

She had to move, had to get out of here. *Oh god, why can't I breathe?*

She gasped for air, hyperventilating, as tears streamed down her face. Feet scrambled across the floor before, gentle but tentative hands, touched her. She shrank away, backpedaling into the chaise, nearly falling in her haste to get away.

"Amelia, it's okay," Gage soothed.

She shook her head. "No. Don't touch me."

"Ok. I won't touch you." He fumbled with the remote, sending a signal to Gareth. "Don't move, honey, there's broken glass on the floor." Gage wasn't even sure she'd heard him.

Running footsteps and a quiet oath signaled Gareth's arrival.

Amelia wrapped her arms around her middle, barely aware of the hurried footsteps approaching. She tried in vain to control her sobs, but all she managed was to muffle the sounds.

"What's—"

"Watch the glass," Gage cautioned.

In spite of the warning, glass crushed beneath her shoes.

"Oh, Amelia." Gareth's voice was full of compassion.

Strong but familiar arms closed around her, sweeping her off her feet.

Amelia struggled against the embrace before the scent of sage, sandalwood, and man wove through her senses. She ceased fighting. Gareth. He wouldn't hurt her.

But he wasn't Joshua.

"What happened?" Gareth asked.

"We were just sitting there, laughing and eating cake, then she started crying," Gage said.

Gareth carried her inside, murmuring into her hair. She trembled, curling into his larger body. Hating how a single smell could debilitate her. She, a strong woman, who'd withstood the rigors of law school using a combination of eBooks and braille, who had to prove her worth every time she walked into a conference room or courtroom, who was every bit as good, if not *better* than her sighted colleagues. She who was surviving the grief of the one man who meant more than her entire life... But one whiff of sweet rot and she was helpless, breathless, and scared.

A soft slide of material, a faint grunt, then a blanket wrapped it around her.

She closed her eyes, savoring the mink soft texture. It soothed her, infusing warmth into her chilly skin. "I'll clean up out here." With that, the terrace doors closed with a snap.

"You're okay, sweetheart."

She shook her head. How could she explain to him she would never be okay? That no matter how well he cared for her, protected her, he could never take the place of her Joshua. Instead she said, "He was here."

"Who was here?" His tone was cautious.

"How did he get in? The man who attacked me...how did he get in?" Even to Amelia's own ears, she sounded hysterical. In an effort to calm down, she rubbed the blanket against her cheek.

"Only you and Gage were outside."

She thumped a fist on his chest. "I smelled him! He was here!"

"Okay. Don't move." Muscles bunched and shifted as he leaned forward, setting her on the couch, but she clung to him, refusing to release her hold as her breath continued to hitch, coming in short, ragged gasps.

He couldn't let her go. Not when that man, the one who hurt her was still out there running loose.

Gareth moved again, this time managing to settle her on the sofa next him. He drew the blanket closer around her, keeping his arm over her shoulders. She gripped his hand.

"All right. You're safe here. I'm just going to have a look around." He stood.

He can't leave me alone. She grabbed his hand in an effort stop him. The blanket pooled at her waist. "You promise I'm safe?" She managed between sobs.

Once more, his scent—sandalwood and man—surrounded her. He lowered himself until he was in front of her, the blanket once more draped over her shoulders.

"Yes, you are. Just breathe with me." He cupped her face, clearing her tears with his thumbs. "C'mon, Amelia. In and out. That's all." He placed her hand on his chest, And he inhaled. "Do what I do, baby."

She struggled to follow his instructions, each stuttered breath punctuated by a sob. He held her close without crowding her. Slowly, her mind settled, and the band tightening her chest loosened. Once her breath evened out, he still continued the deep rhythmic breathing. Amelia was grateful for that.

Now, tears of gratitude burned in her eyes, and she quickly blinked them away. Concern radiated from the man, and she was sure he was anxious to see what had triggered her. But from past experience, he wouldn't leave until she was calm. Her throat was raw, but her mind had finally settled, though the rest of her wanted to curl up into a ball and sleep. Or maybe the sweet oblivion of her rope. She drew in a large breath and slowly exhaled. Yes, she would do that. "I'm all right." She pulled the blanket tightly around her.

"I'll be right back." His sure footfalls echoed away.

Warm, humid air swept into the air-conditioned room, but still she shivered within the cocoon of blankets. She focused on her breathing as she listened to the low murmur of male voices. Would Gareth find anyone out there? Did he even believe her or just think she was losing her mind?

What a sight she had to be. Always poised in public and the courtroom, but here...she was an anxiety-filled, sobbing mess. All because of Joshua.

Sure footsteps returned. "I did a quick look and only found some blood," Gareth said as the cushion dipped next to her.

He uncovered her feet, inspecting the soles. "I was afraid of that."

Only then did pain radiate from her heel to her nerve endings. She jerked her foot away. "Ow. What are you doing?"

"You have a sliver of glass in your foot." Gareth glanced around for tissue or even a clean cloth. There wasn't one. He shifted to stand when the sliding doors whispered open.

At that moment, Gage entered the room carrying a dustpan and broom. His gaze dropped to Amelia's bloody foot and he grimaced. "Is it bad?"

Gareth shook his head. "No, but it'll leave a little scar. Could you bring the first aid kit on your way back?" He gently set her foot down, then went to retrieve a bowl of warm water.

Gage reappeared with the blue waterproof box with the big red "T" on the front. "Um, would you like me to grab you another slice of cake?" Gage set the container next to Gareth on the sofa.

"That would be really nice," she said.

"Be back," Gage called as he left the room.

"What happened?" she demanded as soon as they were alone. "Did you find anything?"

Gareth tended to her wound, cleansing her foot with the water, then patting it dry with a towel. He wouldn't lie to her, but there was something amiss. He frowned as the cut continued to ooze. "We didn't find anyone out there."

"He was there, Gareth."

"I know. Gage smelled it too." Gareth pressed a gauze pad on the cut, then used tape to keep it in place. "Amelia, I don't have all the answers to what's going on, but I promise you…I will find out who is trying to hurt you."

Chapter Four

Joshua Hastings prowled his office. Gray industrial carpet muffled his tireless footsteps. Three years. Three long, horrific, lonely years. He paused long enough to twist the platinum band on his left ring finger. How many times had he thought to discard it as she'd discarded him? He tugged at the band now but still could not bring himself to drag it over his knuckles and throw it away.

With a huff, he stomped back toward the window, staring into the distance, watching the heat waves shimmering from the inky black asphalt or the low hedges marking the perimeter of the parking lot.

He absently rubbed the indent high on his left pectoral near the collarbone. An ache leftover from another life. He rubbed and thought about *her*.

Not knowing fueled him. Anger and hatred fed the fire. Hurt and love threatened to dismantle the foundation of loathing and stroked his obsession of needing to know. Why had she done this to him?

He swung back to his desk, covered in paper, then to the white board; 8x10 glossy headshots of Leigh Olsen, Chad Peter Tyler, and Victor Grimaldi were taped to the surface. Beneath each photo was pertinent information and their relationship to Amelia. These three were involved in some way; he just wasn't sure how.

A knock preceded a friendly baritone. "I'm looking for Joshua Hastings."

"Back here," he called, keeping his eyes on the board. He knew Leigh. Amelia's half-sister. They shared a mother, but Leigh's father had started the law firm Amelia now owned.

He went to his desk, rifled through papers until he found what he wanted. "Leigh had her license, but she no longer practiced, leaving the firm to marry her first husband without a prenup. That left a nice dent in her finances when the two of them split after less than two years into the marriage.

He caught the slight tap and slide. The sound was familiar, yet he was unable to place it. He walked back to the white board and added a notation.

"I hope you don't mind my intruding." The newcomer paused at the threshold, holding a long white cane, one end resting about two feet from his shoulder, the other end sporting a rounded tip, no bigger than a golf ball.

"Not at all," Joshua said. "How may I help you?" He studied the older man: salt and pepper hair, more salt than pepper, creased walnut colored skin and a wide affable smile. He was dressed in pressed jeans, worn sneakers, and a pale blue polo shirt that faded into a dull gray and a stain resembling a ketchup.

"I believe I can be of some service."

Joshua met the man's gaze; The stranger's eyes were brown with a blue ring around the irises. "Do I know you?"

He smiled, a gold-capped eyetooth winking in the late afternoon sun. "I know your wife."

"You are mistaken. I'm divorced."

The older man had the grace to blush. "I'm sorry. Sometimes, I see things before they happen. Amelia and I are friends."

Joshua set down the erasable marker with a click. "Just who exactly are you?"

"Swift Time, Father Time Detective Agency."

Joshua almost laughed. Surely, this wasn't the man's name.

"I get that reaction a lot," he answered the unspoken question. "My parents did a lot of acid and thought it would be cute to have a child named Swift. I took a lot of beatings on the playground."

"Is this a professional call?" Joshua thought it was better to be direct than engage in small talk. Some parents really knew how to complicate their kids' lives.

"Not at all."

"State your business. Time. My patience is growing thin."

Time frowned. "That's the problem with you young folks. Don't know how to have a decent conversation and possibly learn something from their elders."

Joshua dragged his fingers through his hair, the strands flittered round his shoulders. "Would you care to sit?"

"Thanks." Time stood where he was. "Amelia needs you."

He bit back a brittle laugh. "Amelia has a new husband. She doesn't need me."

Frowning, Time rubbed his temples. "Not for long. Lies. Secrets. You need to look beyond all of this and save her."

Old are not, professional courtesy or not, Joshua had enough. He crossed the room, took Time by the arm, and led him out. "I've had enough of you."

Before Joshua realized what happened, Time grasped his wrist, turned into his weight and hip-tossed him to the floor.

"Don't ever manhandle me again. I'm trying to tell you something to save my dear friend." Time straightened his clothes.

Joshua slowly regained his footing, keeping a wary eye on the man.

"Stubborn man. I'll tell Amelia myself." With unerring ability, Time left the office.

Joshua was still standing there when his partner, Dakota, walked in a few minutes later.

"I just passed Father Time in the hall," Dakota said. "What did he want?"

"Father Time?"

"Yeah. The world's oldest professional wrestler." Dakota set down the bag of food. "He's all over YouTube. He travels all over the state, giving motivational speeches to kids. The man has survived cancer, strokes. Did I mention he is blind?"

"Yeah, ya did." Joshua turned to the bag, opened it, and retrieved his sandwich. "You some sort of fan?"

"I love wrestling. My faves are Father Time and Perfect Storm, but I digress. Did he want to hire us?"

Joshua shook his head. "Nope. Turns out, he's a friend of Amelia's."

Late in the evening, several days later, Gareth and Gage sat beneath a weeping willow. Sunlight filtered through the long hanging branches, casting shadows on the lush grass beneath.

"So what's so important that we had to come out to the back forty? Gage scooped a handful of stones, then skipped them across the small stream of water. A smile touched his lips. "I remember the first time you brought me here."

Gareth grinned. "You had to be about four or five."

Gage tossed another stone. "And even then, you were larger than life."

"You were the little brother I was surprised to get."

He snorted. "Like our mother hasn't told that story dozens of times. As I recall, she and father call me a rather fond souvenir." Another stone skipped across the top of the water several times before plunking into the shallow depths. "There were times father would look at me like I wasn't his."

Gareth straightened. "What?

"When I was growing up, I would catch him studying me like I didn't belong to the family. Like he was searching for some flaw."

"But you look just like him," Gareth argued. "Except for the eyes."

"Yes, now I do, but not when I was ten or even fifteen." He looked around for more stones. Finding none, he turned and settled on the grass beside Gareth. "And I'm much lighter than the rest of you."

Gareth would've laughed if his brother wasn't so serious. "Have you looked through the family photo album lately? If anyone's paternity should be questioned, it would be mine. No one on either side is dark as cocoa."

"It's not only the photo album." Gage plucked at a blade of grass. "I overheard Father talking to someone. He thought for the longest time Mother had gotten pregnant by another man when they engaged in some, ah—marital spice."

"When did you hear this?"

Gage shrugged. "I must have been eight or nine. It was only when I was a teenager that I understood what they meant." He managed a sheepish smile. "I liked seeing our parents when they were home. As long as I was quiet and didn't call attention to myself, they let me stay in the room. Then again, they'd forget I was there."

Gareth shifted.

"Spill. You know something."

Gareth shook his head. "I'd have to do some research, Gage. A lot of pieces are falling into place."

"Did you know our parents were swingers or whatever they call themselves?"

Gareth didn't answer.

"And if our parents are so out there, why do they give you such a hard time about being gay?"

A mixture of sadness and longing crossed Gareth's face. If Gage hadn't been watching his brother, he'd have missed the shift from melancholy to affection.

Gareth ruffled Gage's hair. "You ask a lot of good questions. Unfortunately, I don't have an answer for you other than me liking men doesn't fit with their view of what a man should be. Or rather...who their heir-apparent should be." The last was said with cold bitterness.

"They're hypocrites."

"If they are, what does that make me for not living in the open?"

Gage stared at him. "You're the only one who can stand up to them. It's almost like they're afraid of you."

"You have the same strength, Gage. Don't ever forget that."

They fell into companionable silence.

"So why did you bring me out here?"

"I'm taking Victor away for a few days, but I don't want to leave Amelia."

"Are you sure leaving without her right now is wise? Our parents just stopped sniffing around your lifestyle. And you know, Dawson is their personal spy when they're not in residence."

"That's the thing. She's agreed to cover us, but..."

"You need someone to keep an eye on her while you two sneak off for parts unknown."

Gareth nodded. "That's not the only reason I'm asking." He removed a folded card from his pocket, then passed it over.

Gage carefully unfolded the stiff vellum, thinking it was some sort of invitation. His eyes widened at the blood red word. His gaze flew to Gareth's. "Someone's trying to kill her?"

Gareth nodded, his jaw tight.

"Who would want to hurt her? She's one of the good people in this world." His tone was incredulous.

"I don't know who, but I intend to find out."

Amelia loosely held the hand grips of the elliptical. The leash on her wrist moved back and forth, but the dog, tethered to the other end, laid quiet and ready.

Gage kept pace on the treadmill beside her. "Mind if I ask a personal question?" he asked.

"Depends on how personal?"

He grinned. "It's about your panic attacks."

Amelia was silent for several beats. "They're no fun," she finally said.

"No, they're not."

Several more moments passed. Panting and the rhythmic hum of the cardio equipment filled the silence.

"So what's your question?"

"How do I help you through them, if you happen to have one while he's gone?"

The sincerity in his voice caught her off-guard. She slowed her pace, turning her head toward his general direction, catching the slightest hint of movement. "Staying calm is important."

"Okay."

"And getting me to breathe again."

"During the last one, you didn't want me to touch you."

She shrugged. "Wrap me in a blanket before you touch me." She stopped, then stepped off the machine. He stopped as well.

"You never had panic attacks before," he said.

She chuckled as she blotted her face with a towel. "I did, but they were never this bad."

He lifted her hand and placed a bottle of water in her palm. "So what changed?"

She squeezed the bottle, her entire body tensing at the question. Her chest tightened, and for a brief moment, the scents of sweat and rubber seemed to fade. She sucked in a great breath, then slowly blew it out. "I'd rather not talk about it." Even to her ears, her voice sounded thin and frail.

He guided her to a nearby bench. "I'm sorry. I didn't mean to pry. Sometimes...I'm too curious for my own good."

"You'd make a good attorney."

As if sensing her anxiety, Kiska licked her fingers. Amelia rewarded the animal with a scratch behind the ears.

"You know I'd rather play music than research or argue case law," he grumbled.

"Well if you change your mind, your name is already on the door," she teased.

He laughed. "I'll let you and big bro take on the corporate bad guys."

"Speaking of your big bro, how did Gareth bribe you into hanging out with me?" She raised the water to her lips, swallowed, then replaced the cap. "Your presence is appreciated, but I don't need a babysitter."

His laugh was easy, but Amelia heard a slight edge. "Are he and Victor doing okay?"

"They've been a little strange for a couple weeks now."

"Gareth has been working some pretty long hours at the firm lately, then there's my grandmother's bequest."

Gage hesitated, then said, "I don't think that's it. Gareth can deal with that stuff in his sleep. No, there's an underlying thread of tension between the two."

"I thought I was imagining things."

"No, love, your BSP is working just fine."

"BSP?" she repeated.

"Blind Sensory Perception."

She laughed. "Is that what they're calling it now?"

He joined her laughter. "I just made it up."

"You are so silly."

"Can I ask another question?"

"You're full of curiosity today," she mused.

"It's about Joshua."

Her humor faded, replaced by a deep longing and sadness. "He was gone way too soon."

"I would watch the two of you together, hoping one day I would be lucky enough to find someone to love me the way the two of you loved each other."

She could only nod, the words lodged in her throat.

"Why did you marry my brother so soon?"

She managed a wan smile. "Because he needed to be free to love who he wanted."

"Oh," Gage said. "But what about you?"

She squeezed his hand. "He keeps me safe."

"What about falling in love for yourself?"

She pushed to her feet. "That type of love only comes along once in a lifetime. There will never be another Joshua."

Victor splashed a liberal amount of amber alcohol into a short, heavy crystal glass. Gareth padded up behind him and placed a beefy hand on his shoulder. Victor closed his eyes relishing the contact.

Everything about the man was big. Big hands, big feet, big...heart.

"Tell me. What's troubling you?" Gareth prompted, kneading the tense muscles in Victor's shoulders. "God, you've got boulders back here."

Victor allowed his head to fall forward as Gareth worked the worst of the knots from his neck. "I..."

Gareth skimmed a kiss across his bare shoulder. "We never used to keep secrets from one another." He slowly propelled Victor to a nearby sofa. It was just large enough for both men. "You've definitely been keeping secrets from me."

Victor closed his eyes. "I don't want to lose you. You and your family are too important. I view them as if they were my own."

Gareth frowned, then brushed a lock of Victor's brown hair from his face. "You talk as if someone has threatened you."

"Not me," he said after a while.

"I see." Gareth held Victor close, breathing in the other man's scent of citrus. "Whatever this burden is, you don't need to carry it alone. We can get through this together. No matter what it is."

"I've done some absolute wretched things, and there's no way for you or anyone else to forgive me."

"Victor, no matter what it is or how much it costs to get out of it, I will help you." *If I have to dig and find out what you're hiding myself, I will not be pleased.*

"You're already too close."

"I had a rather interesting conversation with my brother before we left on our little trip here."

Victor stiffened, not sure where Gareth was going.

"We discussed my parents and how he overheard some rather...interesting facts regarding his conception."

Oh shit. Gareth knows the truth. Victor's heart hammered in his chest. And that meant Gage knew the truth too. He moistened his dry lips but couldn't force words out.

"These kinds of secrets have a way of losing their power when they come to light." Gareth sighed. "Did you know someone tried to kill Amelia?"

At that, Victor stilled. He swallowed hard, visibly shaken.

"What if something happens to you or my brother," Gareth said.

Victor went a sickly gray beneath his tan. "There's no way to stop what's happening."

"Then, tell me what it is, and let me figure out a solution. We've done the impossible before. There's no doubt it can be done again.

"I started gambling again."

"How much do you owe?"

Victor shook his head. "They didn't want money. Well... at least not my money."

"They didn't want..." Gareth sat up. "What did they want?"

"Information."

"What kind?"

Victor pinned him with bloodshot eyes. "You have to believe me; I didn't know how far he would take this."

"You're talking in riddles again."

Victor pushed up and paced. "Don't you see? If I tell you anything of what I've done, he'll kill you, Gage, and Amelia."

Gareth hissed out a breath. He stood, then blocked Victor's path. "Come with me."

There was only one way to get through to Victor.

Not sure what Gareth had in mind, Victor followed. They walked down a short, carpeted hallway and came to a heavy door at the end. Gareth produced a key from his pocket and unlocked the door. He held the door open, then motioned for Victor to move in.

With some trepidation, the smaller man crossed the threshold, then stopped in his tracks with a gasp. In the center of the room was a St. Andrews Cross, and next to that was a padded spanking bench.

Gareth closed and locked the door. He crossed to a table where two large duffle bags sat.

"What is this?" Anticipation and wariness warred with lust.

"You know exactly what this is." Gareth kept his attention on the bags, selecting, then discarding lengths of rope.

Victor walked over to the cross, running his fingers against the wood's smooth grain. He noted that only carabiners hung in place of any cuffs. A shiver of awareness tightened his belly and groin. It had been a long time since he and Gareth played.

"Strip and stretch," Gareth commanded.

The order was low and seductive; Victor rushed to comply. He folded his discarded clothing, then laid them on the nearby bench.

"Hold out your arms."

When Victor complied, Gareth worked quickly, coiling soft cotton around each wrist. Once he was done, Gareth nodded toward the cross. Victor moved onto the small step, trailing the ends of rope from each arm. Gareth secured him to the cross, giving him just enough length to hold in his hands.

Cool air skittered across his naked flesh. Victor closed his eyes, waiting.

He could hear Gareth moving behind him. The soft swish of his clothes as he walked. The faint drag of the zipper teeth as it was opened. The air moved as something was snapped and flicked. He tightened his hands in the rope. And still, he waited.

Would it be soft? Hard? Silky or rough?

Gareth walked to the table and retrieved two more floggers. These held leather tails and provided a bit more sting than thud. He alternated the tails, smiling when Victor moaned again.

He worked from shoulder to buttocks, to thighs and calves, then worked his way up again. He was neither fast nor slow, just a steady rhythm.

Cold, sharp fingers dragged across the exposed flesh of his back, down to each buttock and up again. His breath stilled in his throat at the sensation. He tried to hold still, but the caress prickled sensitive nerve endings. A moan escaped his lips.

Gareth reached around him, switching the claws to his cheek. "You've allowed someone else to dominate your life," he muttered in his ear. "Does what we have mean so little to you?"

Before Victor could respond, Gareth moved away, taking sensation and his heat with him. Victor sagged in disappointment. "No."

Something cool settled on one shoulder, then slid down his spine. He closed his eyes as the flogger barely kissed his back with small light flicks and snaps.

"You asked for time away," Gareth snapped the flogger, leaving a red welt in its place, "and I gave it."

Victor closed his eyes, savoring the sting. Several more snaps and his back heated with the blows. Sweat beaded on his forehead as his cock leapt and pulsed.

"Just us." Gareth flicked his wrist, only satisfied when implement met flesh. He relished the red welts on the tan flesh. However, it wasn't enough. Victor could and would take more.

Gareth paused, just long enough to stroke a hand down Victor's back, hovering over a spot on his shoulder blades that looked slightly raw, but the skin was not broken. He would be mindful of that spot as he continued the play.

Victor leaned his head against one arm, drawing in small sips of breath. "Please don't stop," he pleaded. "It's been so long."

"Indeed it has."

Gareth swung the leather floggers with speed and precision. Each thwack produced a subtle moan from Victor. He closed his eyes, relishing the sting on the pain/pleasure.

For a time, Victor floated, his world narrowing to the implements assaulting and caressing his body. He was aware of Gareth's heat and light touches in between implement changes. How had he'd forgotten how well Gareth could dominate him? Keep him safe?

The strike of cane across the fullness of his buttocks stilled his body. Three more strikes followed before his brain could comprehend the pain. He blew out a breath as Gareth caressed the stripes. He reached between his legs and fondled Victor's now flaccid cock. When had he cum?

"Seems I still know the right combination of pain and pleasure to bring you to orgasm." He chuckled. "Shall I try again?"

"God yes."

Gareth reached up and released his hand from the carabiners, then led him to the wobbly spanking bench. Victor settled on his knees, and Gareth tied the rope to the D-ring in the floor. He then locked Victor's ankles in place.

Victor shimmied on the bench. He wasn't going anywhere until Gareth released him. His heart soared at the prospect.

"Ah, my love, your submission brings me such pleasure." Gareth dragged his fingers along his already sensitized skin.

Victor couldn't stop the shutter wiggling through his body. He clenched his fists, even as his cock hardened to a painful spike.

Coolness touched his rectum a moment before something large and smooth breached the opening. He held his breath as pressure built, and the fullness became nearly unbearable before the toy settled home.

Two quick sharp snaps forced an exhale from his lips.

And then, the toy vibrated. Not just a constant hum, but it jumped and jiggled to some beat Victor didn't comprehend. Combined with the artful slaps and caresses to his ass, he was lost in a sea of sensation.

He didn't even realize he was begging Gareth to let him orgasm until calloused hands closed around his shaft. Only then did his body succumb to the pressure. Fire roared up his thighs, squeezed his sac, and spurted from his cock in hot, ropy bursts.

He laid there, spent and panting. Gareth released him, caressing his ankles and wrists. He tossed a blanket over him.

A moment later, he was lifted and carried into the bedroom. Gareth settled next to him.

Warm oil was worked into the fire that was his back and buttocks. Victor nuzzled deeper into the mattress. Gareth worked without speaking. Victor fisted the blanket in his hands.

All the guilt and pain he'd caused crashed down on him. How had he betrayed Gareth so badly? How had he hurt the man he loved so terribly? Everything he'd done over the last few years made him an ungrateful arse. And here was Gareth caring for him, ensuring his pleasure and comfort was met. What had he done?

A tear slid from his eye and across the bridge of his nose. He opened his mouth to speak, but a sob burst out.

Gareth stilled in his massage. "Victor?"

"I'm sorry."

Gareth pulled the other man into his arms. "It seems we've played a little too hard."

Victor shook his head, wept, and confessed.

So close and yet so far. Gareth stared at the black lettering on the frosted glass door: Hastings Investigations and Security. This had to be a coincidence, but if Victor was telling the truth, how could this company, his friend's company, be so close and yet...so far away?

With a heavy sigh, he pulled open the door.

Cool, dark slate and wood welcomed him into a small, but tidy, waiting room. A low leather sofa and the obligatory coffee table with magazines sat to his right while a three-tiered shelf held green plants. Other than that, there were no other decorations. Not even a receptionist to greet him.

He could almost believe the agency belonged to someone else until a disembodied voice entreated, "Come on back."

Was that him? The honeyed slow drawl was the right timber and cadence. Gareth forced his steps not to hurry, failed and quickened his pace to where the voice emanated. If this was indeed who he thought it was, he had to set things right.

"My assistant called with an appointment," Gareth called back.

A squeak of springs and precise footsteps reached his ears.

Gareth stopped short when a man appeared in the doorway. For a moment, he couldn't breathe. The man in front of him had piercing blue eyes and sandy brown, shoulder-length hair that curled around his collar.

"Have you come to rub my nose in the fact you're sleeping with my wife?" the other man asked.

"It's true," he managed to gasp. "Where have you been all this time?"

The other man looked him up and down, contempt in every line. "Exactly where I've been since the divorce."

"Divorce? What divorce? You were killed in action."

He scoffed. "You're delusional. I'm very much alive, and you knew it."

"Joshua."

Joshua crossed the space and had the other man against the wall, a forearm against his windpipe. "You were my friend. How dare you do this. You come into my place and pretend like you had nothing to do with tearing me away from my Lia."

Gareth didn't struggle, didn't even fight back. "I think I can explain some of what's going on, but you need to listen to me."

"Why?"

"Because someone is trying to kill Amelia."

Chapter Five

"Amelia!" Gage called.

Amelia bent at the waist, placed her palms on the floor, then walked her feet back until she resembled an upside-down V. Her ponytail brushed the mat as she leaned into the stretch.

"Downward dog?" he asked, standing next to her.

"Yep." She brought one foot forward, then shifted into a modified lunge. "I'm almost done."

"Can you listen while you continue your Pilates?"

She nodded.

"Dear Mr. Gage, we are writing to inform you that we have received your application and you have been selected for a slot in our Fall Repository. Congratulations on your achievement."

Amelia straightened, a wide smile on her face. "Oh, Gage, that's fantastic!"

"I'm just so excited. You're the first one I've shared the news with."

She touched his hand. "That's pretty amazing. Weren't there like ten spots and two hundred applicants?"

"Gareth is going to bust. Is he back yet?"

She nodded. "He's down in his workshop. He's been spending a lot of time down there since we returned from our holiday."

Gage frowned. "Really? I didn't think he was working on anything new."

Amelia caressed her dog's head. "I've been down there a few times, and he's got something working. There's metal, wood, and leather all over the place."

Gage snorted. "Must be working on some new toys for you and Victor. I heard one of you broke his favorite flogger."

"That would be Victor. I have been a very good girl lately."

He laughed. "How did you get started in the lifestyle?"

"A dare in high school."

"A dare?"

"Don't sound so surprised. My family didn't want me to do anything because of my vision. So a friend of mine dared me to sneak out and go into this dungeon she knew of, and well…the rest is history."

"Wait. No it isn't."

She laughed. "I found my calling and never looked back." She gently turned him and pushed him toward the door. "Now, go tell your brother the good news. I'll make reservations at your favorite restaurant so we can celebrate in style."

He scooped her in a quick hug before she could protest, then kissed her on the cheek. "You are such an awesome sister-in-law. Wear something in red."

She laughed. "Will do." She crossed to the telephone, even as the door closed.

Gareth stared at the pages spread on his workbench. Out of all the places on his property, this was the one that offered the most privacy. No one came to bother him as it was so far from the main house, other than Victor, Gage, and Amelia; their visits were sporadic. Now, he had a new toy to test; a wicked smile touched his lips. He loved trying out new things on them. Still he preferred to do this business in his own space.

He touched one black and white photo of a man with rugged and chiseled features. His dark hair was longer than before, and those piercing eyes looked a little more haunted. But three years could do that to a man.

Gareth ran a hand over his scalp. Joshua was alive and well. Somehow, Gareth had to find a way to break the news to Amelia. His heart skipped a beat. If he told Amelia the truth, they could annul their marriage, and he could be with Victor. The law firm would continue, and his parents wouldn't dare bring his sexuality into the mix. Not after he knew about them and Victor.

Beep. Beep.

Gareth looked up at the monitor. His brother was fairly skipping down the path. Gareth hurried to put away the file and shoved the papers in his safe just as Gage knocked on the door.

Gareth pulled an unfinished paddle toward him along with a piece of sandpaper. "Come in," he called, dragging the paper over the wood.

"Ah. So you are working."

Gareth ran his fingers over the paddle. "There's a convention in a few months. I've had a few requests."

"Has anyone ever recognized you?"

Gareth grinned. "A few, but mostly they're too afraid to say anything." He rubbed a thumb over the spot he had just sanded. Satisfied with the smoothness, he moved to a different area.

"But you're so well known."

"Which furthers the rumors and innuendoes." Gareth glanced at his brother. "I'm sure you didn't skip all the way down here, just to ask me about toy making."

"I did not skip!" Gage denied.

Laughing, Gareth flipped the paddle over and began sanding the other side. "Wanna give this a try?" he teased.

"Uh, maybe some other time? We are celebrating tonight?" Gage brandished the letter.

"You got in!" He set the wood aside and engulfed his brother in a hug.

"Yes. I start in the fall."

"That is indeed cause for celebration." He walked to the phone mounted on the wall. "Reservations..."

"Uh. Amelia is taking care of those."

"I shoulda known you'd tell her first."

"You're not upset?"

Gareth chuckled. "She has an ear for stuff like that. I'm proud of you, bro."

"What about our parents?"

"You let me handle them. My little brother is going to follow his dreams and be happy doing it."

Gage cringed. "I will make sure I'm scarce on that day. What time is dinner?"

"Probably seven,"

Gareth looked at his watch. "I'm going to run an errand, then I will be back to take everyone to the restaurant."

"Oh no. We are taking a car and getting white girl wasted."

"I'd like to see you convince Amelia into that one." He ushered Gage from the workshop, then locked the door. "She will not walk out drunk."

Gage flashed a wicked grin. "Then she'll just have to be carried."

Laughter flowed as freely as the alcohol. Gareth surveyed the table. Victor sat to his immediate right, while Gage sat opposite Victor and next to Amelia. She was seated in the corner where it was unlikely anyone, but family, would touch her. Kiska laid beneath the table, shifting every now and then when someone's foot came to near.

Gareth smiled. This was his family—the most important people in his life—and he would protect all of them with his life. A hand squeezed his thigh. He glanced to his right.

"You've got a smug look on your face," Victor pointed out.

"I was just thinking how wonderful it is to be surrounded by the people I love."

"Yes," Gage chimed in. "It is an amazing feeling to know we are loved and encouraged for who we are." Gage raised his glass. "I propose a toast." He turned to Amelia and urged, "Raise your glass, Amelia."

Amelia rushed to comply, her movements a little unsteady as she did. The other men held their glasses.

"To Gareth, a true visionary, leader and the best damn big brother ever!"

They clinked their glasses against Amelia's as they echoed the sentiment.

Musical notes interrupted the festivities. Victor shifted beside Gareth. Gareth pressed a hand to Victor's.

"Not tonight," he said. "Let's stay in the moment. Whatever it is, can wait until tomorrow?" He leaned closer. "We have other things to celebrate."

Victor turned slightly, holding Gareth's gaze. "You found a way?"

He nodded. "Of course, but right now, it is Gage's moment. We will celebrate later." He scorched the other man with a glance. "I've got a new toy to try on you."

Joshua stared at the papers scattered across the wide conference table. He still wasn't sure what to make of Gareth's visit. Three years was a long time to make up a lie. Yet one thing was undeniable, Amelia had divorced him.

But was it voluntary? The questioned nagged him.

The Amelia he knew and loved supported him, loved him, cherished him, and waited for him every time he was deployed into action. The last time was to be his last.

He absently rubbed an indentation just below his collarbone. Any lower and he really would've been dead. Only thoughts of Amelia sustained him. And while he was recovering, some slick looking lawyer brandished papers and a cashier's check in his face so that he would walk out of her life. For good.

Sure, the settlement was a tidy sum, but he didn't want Amelia for her money. He wanted her because she made him happy, because he loved her, and he believed she'd loved him.

He bent over one of the spreadsheets Gareth had left him. Frowning, he compared it to a bank statement from the same time period. He grimaced. Someone was skimming funds.

Not a professional job, nor were they greedy, but it was enough to call attention if anyone with a brain was paying attention. And apparently, Gareth was paying attention.

Joshua studied the accounts. The bleed began about three weeks after his divorce and appeared to have stopped about six months ago.

Why hadn't Gareth stopped the hemorrhage sooner? Was it possible Gareth was the one behind the embezzling? Joshua dismissed the notion. Gareth was a lot of things, but he wasn't a thief.

And could he believe the story he told? Could someone only want Amelia out the way for her money? Joshua snorted. That was a stupid question. Amelia was worth millions, even without her grandmother's inheritance. He wondered if she still practiced law or held the controlling interest in the firm.

He walked over to his computer. There was one way to find out.

Wiggling the mouse awakened his computer. He typed in a URL he hadn't visited in years and watched a pretty website populate his screen with cool blue and purple tones.

There she was, soft mocha cream skin, a professional updo, and full generous lips curved in a sweet smile. She was still practicing law and still the primary partner. He surfed the site. Interesting how Bedford came along as a partner after they married. Even more interesting, the partner Bedford replaced seemed to have dropped off the face of the earth.

Joshua returned to Amelia's picture. He studied the photo, a hint of sadness lingering in her irises. His gaze dropped to her throat, to the triangular pendant nestled there.

Why hadn't she taken it off? If she had divorced him, why hadn't she rid herself of that symbol?

Hope spurted, and he ruthlessly wrestled it into submission. Just because she still wore his collar—a symbol of his love and devotion to her as her dominant—it didn't mean anything.

Or did it?

Shaking his head, he scanned the page. Her most recent post was uploaded last night. It was an excerpt from a recent interview.

"The fact we were able to prove copyright infringement on the part of our client is momentous. No one can copyright an idea. If that were the case, every writer out there would be accused of plagiarizing the Bible. I'm sure if the plaintiff had presented the courts with satisfactory documentation, there could've been a different outcome. As it is, we proved our case, and the plaintiff needs to compensate our client."

Straightening, he allowed his gaze to linger on the photo, then slide away to stare out the window.

There had to be a reason, other than greed and money, as to why someone wanted his Amelia dead.

A light drizzle fell the next afternoon. Amelia hummed to herself as she puttered around the massive kitchen. She wasn't much for cooking, but she loved to bake. Right now, she wanted the comfort of making bread. A soft smile touched her lips. Gareth and Gage enjoyed fresh-made bread. Neither of them could wait until the loaves had sufficiently cooled before they cut into them.

She gathered the ingredients, so she could zip through the measurements.

Footsteps thumped through her musings. She lifted her head to listen. The steps were hurried, and if she wasn't mistaken, slightly frantic. She shook her head. Probably nothing.

She measured out flour, sugar, salt, and yeast into a waiting bowl. A phone rang. She ignored that too. Voicemail or the answering machine would pick it up.

Carefully, she poured warm water as she turned on the mixer.

"Amelia?"

Amelia turned off the mixer. Anxiety clung to every letter in her name. "Victor? Is something wrong?"

He panted, as if he'd been running. "Have you seen Gareth?"

"He's in his workshop. Were you just running around?"

"He's not answering his phone." There was definite panic in the man's voice.

Amelia stepped toward Victor. "You know how he is when he's working."

Victor grasped her shoulder. She gasped as his fingers bit into her. "Are you sure he's in his workshop?"

"Yes. You're scaring me, Victor. What's wrong?"

Victor turned and fled the room.

"Victor!" she called after him. "Kiska. Come." Amelia didn't bother with the harness. She moved through the kitchen and through the sliding doors. She made her way down the walk. Ahead of her, she could hear Victor's running footsteps and him calling for Gareth.

The desperation in his voice struck her with dread. "C'mon, girl. Something is really wrong." She hurried forward. Bright splashes of color blurred by her.

A faint whomp filled the silence before the world shattered in a thunderclap explosion. One moment she was standing, the next she was sailing backward by the concussive blast.

Kiska barked. Amelia struggled to her knees, only to sit down again. Running footsteps vibrated the ground. Gentle hands touched her.

"Are you hurt?" Gage demanded.

She shook her head. "Gareth and Victor," she managed to croak.

Foliage and bushes snapped to her right. "I'm too late," Victor said his voice calm.

Gage pressed his phone into her hands. "Call 9-1-1. Victor is injured."

Smoke and the distinct smell of burning wood filled the air. "What's on fire?"

"Gareth's workshop."

"Gage? Where's Gareth?"

Chapter Six

Amelia stood straight and quiet, the leash held loosely in her hand. She was aware of the people around her. Some laughed, some cried, while others engaged in quiet conversations. In other words, their world kept turning.

For the second time in her life, hers had stopped.

"You can't stand here all night," Gage said near her left shoulder.

"If I go in there, it will be real, and I don't want it to be real," Amelia confessed.

Gage coughed. "I know what you mean. But he wouldn't want us to *not* celebrate his life."

She shuttered a breath. "Who took him from us, Gage?"

"Amelia, I'll make you a promise. You help me get through this dinner, and I will help you find who murdered my brother."

"Okay. We have to find Victor."

"Victor is not taking Gareth's death with grace or dignity," Gage replied. He tucked Amelia's hand in the crook of his arm.

"No, he's not. I think he was sedated for the funeral."

Noise and sound enveloped them as they entered Abagail's, a trendy bar owned by a friend and offered for the repast.

Amelia hesitated.

As if sensing her anxiety, Gage patted her hand. "I'll get you settled, then grab you something to eat."

Amelia nodded. Has there been any word from your parents?"

He stiffened beside her. "They've already left the country," he said bitterly. "But your family is in attendance."

"I'm sorry about that."

He placed her hand on the back of a chair. "You're next to Victor. I'll be back with something to eat."

Joshua Hastings tuned out the loud, drunken laughter and good-natured argument over the baseball game blaring from one corner of the bar. Gareth would've been proud at the turnout, that so many were swapping stories amidst a baseball game. He swung his focus to the woman sitting at the opposite end.

She'd let her hair grow. The rich auburn strands just kissed the skin of her mocha latte brown shoulders. Desire burned an unwilling path through his veins and pulsed low. Not a single day went by that he didn't ache for her, miss her. Loved her. Hated her.

For whatever reason, Amelia, the woman whom he loved, respected, dominated, and protected, had divorced him, and married someone else. The knowledge burned in his mind and heart as easily as a brand. He had no warning. Just an attorney and a check for services rendered.

Bitterness tasted like ash, and he washed it down with a swig of water. He had a job to do, and he needed to set his personal feelings aside in order to do it.

Joshua shifted on the hard wooden stool. Just looking at her—the woman who fulfilled his every fantasy—hurt. He'd enjoyed testing her limits, introducing her to new depths of pleasure and just the right amount of pain. He'd accepted her for who she was, never cared that she was wealthy beyond anything he'd ever see. Besides, she never acted like a snobby, rich bitch until she had divorced him.

Not one time did she return his phone calls or messages. When he saw the article announcing her marriage to one Gareth Bedford esquire, a man he used to trust, there was nothing left for Joshua to do except get on with his life. Obviously, Amelia had.

And here he was, three years later, watching his ex-wife exchange pleasantries when she'd just buried her husband. He narrowed his gaze and leaned forward. Funny. She didn't look like a grieving widow. If anything, she was doing more consoling than weeping.

He studied the man sitting on Amelia's right. The man was crying into his beer, his water blue eyes bloodshot and swollen. She rested a hand on his forearm and leaned close. There was something familiar about him, but Joshua couldn't remember where he'd seen him.

The man covered her hand with his, and she flinched, just a barely there gesture that Joshua would've missed if he hadn't been watching.

As if realizing his mistake, her companion quickly removed his hand, reached in his jacket pocket, and wiped his face with a crumpled hanky.

Joshua glanced at his phone and compared the pictures. Victor Grimaldi, Gareth's personal assistant and best friend. Everything he ever wanted to know about the man, and a few he didn't, were at Joshua's fingertips.

Jealousy rippled through his gut when Victor leaned over and gave Amelia a hug. She stiffened before returning the embrace.

He slid off the stool. *Something isn't right.* The Amelia he knew was a loving, giving woman. This one seemed to have an aversion to being touched. Anger bubbled. Who'd hurt her? A wave of protectiveness washed over him, much as it had the first time he'd met her. He breathed deep. Focus on that. Amelia needed someone to protect her now more than ever.

Someone wanted his Amelia dead.

Amelia Hastings-Bedford drummed her fingers on the smooth wood counter, gnawing at her lower lip. She tilted her head to the side, listening to the party. From the sounds of things, Gareth's life was being celebrated in grand fashion. Just the way he would've wanted. She blinked back the tears burning her eyes and blew out a shaky breath.

Saying good-bye to Gareth hadn't been as painful as she expected. Maybe because she was still grieving for someone else. Even now, sitting here, trying to console Victor, she felt the loss of a good friend and not the soul-shattering ache of her heart.

Victor reached over and wrapped her in an awkward hug. She stilled. After a moment, she returned the affection.

"I'm so sorry, Amelia," he murmured, his words slurring. "This is all my fault."

She patted his hand. "It was an accident, Victor. Not your fault." At least, that's what the investigators had told her. Something about faulty wiring, a burned-out plug, and poor ventilation. Gareth died quick and painlessly or as the coroner said, *He just went to sleep.* She wished she could believe his death was just an accident, but too many questions were left unanswered.

"My fault!" Victor repeated. "You should get away while you can."

Amelia rolled her eyes; he's been talking like this all week. Quite frankly, she was ready to call a therapist and have him admitted somewhere for his own good. She didn't have the strength to deal with him and her grief. "I might do that, Vic. A few days of quiet would be welcomed right now."

"I can't believe he's gone."

She couldn't either. How did she tell Victor she felt just at fault? Gareth went to his workshop that day to bring her something he'd found. Whatever it was he had, she'd never know. Some instinct warned her it was what got him killed.

A faint crack rolled through the room before a shout of triumph followed. Apparently, a homer or a base hit must have occurred to yield such a reaction which was enough was enough to momentarily draw her from her melancholy.

"All right," Gage began. "I procured plenty of veggies as well as dip. Both share the twelve o'clockish position. At the three is fruit, at the six is some sort of wrap, and at the nine is chips." He slid the plate in front of her, then placed her hand next to it. "My brother was different."

The sweet scent of carrots, and maybe red bell pepper, reached her nostrils, along with smoked turkey and roast beef. The aromas were enough to tempt her waning appetite.

Amelia laughed. "Indeed he was. He wanted a healthy dinner for us all."

At a momentary lull in surrounding conversations, the hiss of liquid hitting glassware before it swelled was lost in the mist of overlapping voices . From somewhere in the bar, she could make out a printer doing its thing. The chair beside her scraped back.

"If he truly wanted healthy, he wouldn't have asked to have it in a bar."

Amelia nibbled on a carrot. "He didn't expect to go for a long, long time."

Gage sniffled. "I don't know if I can go on without him."

Amelia reached over and grasped his hand. If Gage started crying, she would lose it. They needed to hold their emotions together a little while longer. "He protected us all. He made you trustee of his estate."

He coughed. "How do you know that?"

"Gareth wanted me to know all of his affairs. He didn't want anyone to try and use me again."

Beside her, Victor loosed a sob. "This is all my fault."

"He's a mess," he muttered. "Don't let them serve him anymore alcohol."

"Let Abigail know. She'll make sure he gets water or something other than liquor."

A gentle hand touched her arm. "There you are, Amelia."

Amelia shifted on her stool, turning to face the newcomer. "Oh, Abigail. Thank you so much for offering your place." She hugged the other woman.

"How are you holding up?" Genuine concern lit the other woman's voice as she kept her hand on Amelia's arm.

"Hanging in there." As unobtrusive as she could, Amelia moved her arm until they were no longer touching.

"Did I hear you want me to cut off your friend?" Abigail asked.

"If you would."

"Consider it done. Do you need anything right now? I can bring it to you?"

"I'm good. Gonna eat a bit," Amelia said.

Abigail hugged her again. "Give a holler if you need anything." The tap slide of Abigail's cane was swallowed in the noise and laughter.

"You have some really good friends," Gage commented as the other woman left.

Amelia swiped at her eyes. "I really do. If more people offered their condolences, she would go into pieces. Their sincere words made Gareth's absence not just permanent but wholly real. Gareth was never coming back. Just like her Joshua."

Victor continued to weep.

"Maybe you should see about getting Victor home," she suggested. "Nobody will think less of us if we leave now." Yes, leaving now was good. What little control she possessed over her emotions was fast eroding. Gradual bands constricted her chest. The last thing she needed or wanted was a full-blown anxiety attack.

"I'm sending Carter a text. Finish eating and I'll take Victor for a walk."

Amelia nibbled at the food with no real appetite. She shifted on the stool as Victor leaned into her. She braced a hand on the bar, countering the unexpected weight.

"Easy, old boy," Gage murmured, maneuvering the man from Amelia.

Amelia relaxed but remained alert.

"Just let me be," Victor slurred his words, pushing Gage away.

Clothing rustled, and a light grunt met her ears.

"I can't," Gage said. "My brother wouldn't like it if we left you in this state."

"I'm the reason he's dead," Victor wailed, then abruptly fell silent. Wood scraped across the floor as several nearby people gasped.

"Victor?" Amelia cried. She was nearly knocked off her stool as a heavy weight fell against her, then slid to the floor.

"He's just passed out," Gage assured her.

Amelia settled down again. "I'll get him to the car." He grunted as he hoisted Victor into a fireman's carry." He's gonna have one mother of a hangover when he finally wakes up."

She placed a hand on Gage's arm before he could leave. "Stay with him. He shouldn't be alone when he finally wakes."

"Yeah. Carter is coming this way."

"Thanks." She placed her napkin on her plate Before gathering her purse.

"Mrs. Bedford?" She turned toward the voice. "It's Carter, ma'am."

"Oh yes." She slid off the stool. "Gage said you were here."

"Yes, ma'am. He wouldn't let me assist him with Mr. Grimaldi. He told me to make sure you made it into the car. Would you like me to have someone wrap your plate for you?"

She shook her head. "No, I really just need some air."

"Of course," he said. He threaded her hand through the crook of his arm.

Allowing someone other than Gareth to guide her still bothered her. She clicked her tongue. "C'mon, Kiska." She bent at the knees and grasped the handle of the harness on her guide dog. She untangled her hand from Carter and gave Kiska the commands to lead her out.

Colors blurred in front of her eyes. The noises bled into one giant buzz of conversation. Fried foods, yeast, stale sweat all blended into au d' restaurant and should've been impossible to smell anything else. And yet…a scent, like the forest after a hard rain, so subtle it halted her steps. The dog tugged, but she held fast. Tears clogged the back of her throat. She missed him so much. It was hard to believe it had been three years since she buried her Joshua.

Carter touched her sleeve, and she moved forward. Joshua was gone. Just like Gareth. She choked back a sob. Now was not the time to fall apart. She could do that in the privacy of her bedroom, but she would not breakdown and weep in public.

The warm, humid night was a welcome change from the chilly air conditioning. She paused on the sidewalk, just long enough to draw a deep lungful of air.

"Are you okay?"

She smiled at the concern in Carter's voice. "As well as can be expected. I'm really looking forward to home and quiet."

"I understand. Mr. Bedford will be missed."

"Do you mind if we walk around a bit before we get into the car?"

"Of course not."

She listened to her surroundings. Gareth used to bring her to this particular bar, not because it was owned by her friend Abagail, but its proximity to her favorite place. A walking park which held a fountain and plenty of flowers. The wide paving stones made it easy for her to navigate. Between the intermittent traffic, she could hear the faint splash of water.

The dog's nails clicked on the cement, followed by Carter's tread a few paces behind her. She appreciated that. He didn't crowd her as some of the other staff did. Gradually, the flow of water grew louder, and a breeze blew the scent of chlorine—softened by a myriad of floral and rich loam mingle with—she sniffed—tobacco.

She frowned. Smoking wasn't allowed within the park, but the odor was so faint, maybe it blew in from one of the ashcans at the entrance.

A low growl emanated from the dog, brushing against her knees. She stopped. "Kiska? What is it?" She listened, unable to hear the driver's footsteps. "Carter?"

Stale smoke and fetid body odor assailed her nostrils. Quick heavy footfalls were her only warning before arms grabbed her from behind. She screamed. The canine barked and growled at her attacker. *I need to get away!*

Dragging her heel along his shin, she stomped on his instep. He howled and shoved her away. Amelia stumbled forward; pavement grated against her right leg while her hands absorbed the rest of the impact. The shock registered to every part of her body. She had to get up. Get moving.

"Help!"

Swearing filled the air behind her. The dog was growling. A howl ripped the air. Kiska must have bitten one. She moved to her knees. An arm curved around her throat, and she was jerked to her feet. Flashes of light snapped behind her lids as her body fought for oxygen. There was no time to panic if she wanted to live. The arm tightened more.

A quick elbow jab to her assailant's rib loosened his hold. She gripped the fingers of the hand encircling her throat and bent them as far back as she could. An audible snap filled the air. Still holding his hand, she spun, jerked her attacker forward and caught him in the face with her knee. When he went limp, she released him and stepped back.

Hands raised, stance wide, she waited. Listening. Heavy breathing. A groan. Kiska's low growl. Someone else was there. Footsteps crunched. Air shifted. Tension knotted. The sudden intake of breath.

She shifted but not fast enough. Pain exploded across her cheek, and she was knocked to the ground. Her head snapped sideways. The metallic taste of blood exploded across her tongue, but she fought back. She would not go quietly. Her attacker straddled her chest, grabbed her flailing arms, and pinned them above her head. Something cold and metal pressed to her throat. She stilled.

"You're going to call that damn dog off and not give me anymore trouble. Understand?"

She concentrated on his voice. Low, gravelly but she couldn't tell if it was because he was whispering, out of breath, or both.

"Call the dog off."

"You're crushing me." She managed to gasp. His weight eased a fraction from her torso, just enough for her to fill her lungs and scream. A hard smack cut the sound short. Stars danced before her vision, and she whimpered.

Footsteps vibrated through the ground, and a heartbeat later, a grunt and cursing filled the air as the weight left her body. Amelia rolled to her side. "Kiska." She clicked her tongue. "C'mere, girl." A cold wet nose brushed her neck. She ran her hands over the animal, searching for any injuries. She was damp in a couple of places but nothing serious. "Let's find Carter and get out of here."

An engine gunned, the slide of metal on hinges preceded the squeal of tires. "Let's go!" a male voice shouted.

Footsteps pounded past. She tensed, tangling her fingers in Kiska's fur. The dog growled but didn't leave her side. The vehicle sped off, and she blew out a breath. The animal relaxed, then nudged her.

"Right. Right. We need to get help and Carter." She slowly stood, her body protesting the move. She stumbled, and a hand grasped her arm. *Someone else?* She jerked away, throwing a punch. Her fist was caught, and the smack was loud in the silence.

"I'm not going to hurt you. Relax."

The voice was warm, confident, and it slid over her like maple syrup. She stood still. Something about the cadence of those sensuous tones left her needy. It had to be all the emotions from the attack.

"You're safe with me." His words rang with truth.

His voice. It seemed so familiar, and yet...it shouldn't. "I'm blind. Two men. At least...I think it was just two. They attacked me, and I'm afraid they've done something to my driver. Do you see him anywhere?"

"My partner is tending to him. He was hit over the head. He'll be just fine. Let's take a look at you, though."

Gentle fingers cupped her cheek. The contact sent a tingle down her spine. She held her breath as he swiped his thumb across the fullness of her bottom lip. It was an entirely intimate gesture. She pulled away, only to be grabbed around the waist and held in place.

Any other time Kiska would be growling, but she sat calmly, as if waiting. "Who are you?" She forced the words past her lips. The hand at her waist brought her closer. Her breasts touched the solid wall of his chest on each exhale.

His scent, an alluring blend of man and musk, slammed into her, jogging memories that she'd buried deep. She curled her fingers around his biceps as her knees went soft. He held her close; his strong arm and the grip on his muscles were the only thing holding her upright. The day had been trying, and now, her senses were going crazy.

"What's the matter, Lia?" His breath tickled the delicate shell of her ear, tightening her nipples.

No one called her that anymore. Surrounded by this man's scent and his soft Southern drawl, all she could think about was the way his lips whispered over her skin. How his fingers would send her into oblivion, and how he always made her feel—cherished, as if she was the most precious thing in the world.

She swallowed the tears clogging her throat. Those days were long gone, buried in a grave and hidden in her heart where no one could erase his memory. "Who are you?"

"You've forgotten me already?" Bitterness and anger hardened his voice. She stepped back. "Did I mean so little to you?"

She moved her hands to his chest. *I am losing my mind. Someone is playing a very, cruel joke here.* "Please. I don't know who you are."

The hand at her cheek drifted to her hair, tangled in the strands, and pulled her head back. Strong fingers massaged her scalp. She was dreaming. That was the only sane explanation. She must've hit her head when she fell, and now… she was having some sort of episode.

She had to know. Amelia drifted her hands over his face. A scruffy beard prickled her fingertips. He rubbed his cheek to her palm. *This...this can't be right.* Her heart clenched. It was familiar, too familiar.

"I-it can't be."

"Why not? What did you find so abhorrent about what we shared, that you couldn't tell me to my face?"

She sucked in a breath. The voice. The scent. The hand moving in her hair. When his lips grazed the long-forgotten scar near her temple, she forgot to breathe.

"Why not, Lia?"

"Because you're dead."

Chapter Seven

Her head was swimming, but she was warm and comfortable. For the first time in years, Amelia felt at peace. Fingers stroked her hair, while the silk of her sheets caressed her naked flesh. A sigh parted her lips, and she settled more soundly into the sweet haven of the body wrapped around hers.

She reached out a hand and trailed her fingers over a solid wall of muscle. So familiar. If she were dreaming, she could indulge her senses a little longer. Rough, calloused hands skimmed her body, dragging the sheet down, exposing her nipples to cool air.

A hand returned to cup her breast, teasing the pebbled peak with care. She stretched, enjoying the attention. Warm, moist lips followed, gently sucking the tip. Heat trickled between her thighs.

She brought a hand to the back of his head. Long strands tickled her skin. She flexed her fingers, grasped a handful, and jerked.

"Ow. What was that for?" A hard masculine body pinned her to the bed. His erection settled at the apex of her thighs; the only barrier was the sheet.

The recent events rushed back to her memory, and she stilled her struggles. "You...we..." Aches rippled through her body. The attack had been real. Pain seemed to dance along her nerve endings. "Please, get off me."

When he rolled from her, she sat up and moved to the edge of the bed. Her muscles were tight and sore as she stood. She dragged a hand through her tousled hair. Wait. She was naked. *When did that happened?* Not that she minded being in the nude, but she didn't remember taking off her clothes. Panic knotted her belly, and she clenched her hands at her side.

She whirled on her heel. "What did you do?" Fear made her voice higher than usual. "What did you do to me?" Fabric rustled. Soft footfalls neared, and she stumbled back.

"Lia, what's wrong?"

Heat enveloped her. "You're not real," she shouted.

He grasped her hands and placed them on either side of his face. "Lia, I'm very much alive."

She shook her head and snatched her hands away. "No. I buried you. Just like I buried Gareth." He cupped her cheek, and she jerked. "Don't touch me."

"Lia."

Her heart raced; her breath came in pants. She could actually hear the blood pounding in her ears. Why couldn't she breathe? She clenched her hands into fists as she willed her body to stop trembling.

"Lia." His voice was gentle, barely above a whisper. "I promise. I'm very much alive, but I need you to calm down right now." Something warm wrapped around her shoulders.

"Just breathe with me for a moment."

"I can't...I can't..."

He cupped her face. "Listen to me." One hand lingered on her cheek while the other pressed her palm to his chest. The beat of his heart thumped strong and sure. "Just follow my lead. In and out. Slow breaths." She shook her head, tears streaking down her cheeks. He swiped one away with his thumb. "You're fine. Just breathe with me."

Joshua smoothed her hair from her face. She resisted, tugging her hand from beneath his. Her Joshua was dead. She had the papers, the pretty flag, and the medals to prove it. But the man in front of her refused to release her, even smelled just like him. Tasted like him. Sounded like him.

Even as her mind struggled to comprehend the changes, her heart understood. Her trembling subsided, and though he was no longer touching her, she kept her hand on his chest. Her fingers slid over his skin. His pecs were chiseled and well defined; although one pec held an indent large enough to accommodate two fingers. This had to be a new wound. She didn't remember it being there before. Tears pricked her eyes. What had happened to him to cause this injury?

She worried her bottom lip as she drifted down his torso. There would be a rough patch just at the bottom of his ribcage, when he'd taken shrapnel. Tears seeped beneath her lids as her fingers skimmed the flesh, now the texture of a cheese grater.

Amelia circled him, discovering old scars and new ones. She leaned her head between his shoulder blades. A stuttered breath wobbled past her lips. "Why?" Hot tears slid down her cheeks, pooling beneath her chin. "Why would someone do this to me? To us?"

"I don't know." The words vibrated through his chest.

"Are we still married?"

"No." His tone was harsh and clipped.

She stepped away, tossing aside the blanket he'd placed over her shoulders during her hysterics. "Did Gareth know you were still alive? Did you tell him to marry me?"

Joshua faced her, his gaze taking in her tear-stained face. The hardest thing he'd done was stand there while she explored his body or allow her to leave the bed when she'd been so receptive to his attention. Good thing she was standing behind him. He didn't want to scare her with his raging hard-on.

"I did not tell Gareth to marry you. He had instructions to play when you needed to play but not take over my role."

Her full lips formed a small 'o.'

"How long did you wait before you jumped into bed with another man, Amelia?" He kept his tone deliberately calm, while inside, he was still seething.

She flinched, as if she'd been struck. "I didn't jump into bed with anyone."

He touched the thin silver necklace at her throat, grasped it in his hand, intending to yank it from her neck. The mere sight of the jewelry mocked him.

Her fingers brushed his wrist "Don't. Please don't. I never took it off, and he never put on another one." The plea in her voice struck a nerve.

He pulled the chain away, inspecting the small dangling heart and dropped it as if it burned. All these years...she'd never taken it off. He cleared his throat. "Why not?"

Her dark eyes glistened as they shifted from side to side. "Because I loved you more than anything in this world, and sometimes, it was the only thing keeping me from crawling into the plot next to yours." She stared in his general direction, then lowered her head. "I'd have mourned you forever if I could have."

"Why didn't you?" He circled her, admiring her lush curves, disliking the bruises forming on her flesh from last night's altercation. Had she lost weight? He tilted his head, studying her medium-built frame. She was average in height, toned, but with all the sinful voluptuousness of bygone era pin-up girls. A gasp stuck in his throat when he focused on her back. Thin raised welts crisscrossed her beautiful mocha skin.

Fury burned in his gut. Was this how Gareth treated her? If the man wasn't dead already, he'd kill him. Joshua reached out and traced one. She flinched. "Hold still." His voice was harsher than he intended. She quivered beneath his touch but did not move. The marks weren't fresh. Someone had done this to her. He followed the lines from her shoulders to the rounded globes of her sweet derriere.

"Did he do this to you?" He gripped her shoulders and turned her to face him.

She shook her head.

He held her by her arms and dragged her close. "Did he mistreat you?"

"No."

"Amelia."

"I don't know."

She paled, and her breathing was ragged again. He folded her in his embrace. "All right. All right." The last thing he wanted was to send her into a full-blown anxiety attack. He held her until she calmed, and her breathing returned to normal. "Did he hurt you?"

Her hair moved against his chest. "No. Never without my permission."

He resisted a smile at the humor in her voice. "Then who hurt you without your permission?"

"I don't know."

Amelia tried to pull away, but he held fast, stroking the curve of her spine. The strong th-thunk of his heart vibrated beneath her ear. She slowly released an exhale and allowed him to lift her in his arms.

Once more, something warm wrapped around her as he settled her in his lap. She leaned her head on his shoulder. Cradled in his lap, she could almost forget the last three years. Forget that awful moment when she was helpless and alone.

"What happened?"

"Our playtime went wrong." She moved to get off his lap, but his arms tightened. Another stuttered breath. "We'd finished one of the demos at the Vet Con."

"The one the club holds every year?" he asked.

She nodded. Yes, "I wanted—needed to feel something other than this soul-sucking despair. So I went to Gareth. We hammered out a scene. Victor and Gareth would spot me, and all parties were happy." She paused. "We settled on an hour and if I was still okay, longer, but two hours was the max. After thirty minutes, I wanted to stop. I felt off, like I was coming down with the flu or something. He said, 'okay.' He wasn't feeling well either, so we could continue another day. I remember a knock, a thud I think, and things go a little hazy from there."

Fingers stroked her hair. "Something else, Lia. I see it on your face."

She shook her head, unable to voice the abuse done to her.

"Yes. It may have been awhile, but it's there. No secrets."

She slid off his lap, the blanket pooling at her feet. "Where were you?" She dashed at the tears streaking down her cheeks. "Why did you have to leave me alone? Why didn't you steal me away?"

"When I got the paperwork, you were already married. There wasn't much I could do at that point." His voice was hard.

"I don't understand, Joshua. Who would take you away from me?"

"Your family never liked me." Disdain filled his statement.

She'd gone against her family's wishes when she married Joshua—choosing love over power and prestige. But he also made her feel safe. Something she hadn't felt since he left. Though he always ensured she had care during leave on his assignments, she never had that same sense of security until he was back in her arms. This last time...she swallowed hard. He hadn't come home.

"I'm sure they'd have no problem perpetuating a lie to get whatever they wanted from you." The statement sliced through her thoughts.

Amelia paced the expanse of room. "It's been three years. Surely you could've gotten a message to me."

"I sent messages. I phoned and even came by."

She stopped moving and swung around her mouth agape. "You were in my room. I thought I was dreamin'..."

Joshua studied Amelia's naked form. Desire burned low, and all he wanted to do was erase the last three years. But there was still so much between them. She divorced him and married someone else. Maybe that was the part he was having trouble with; how could she not have known what she was signing? And who told her he was dead?

He followed her movements as she crossed the room and stood in front of a large window. She lifted her face, her features disappearing in the glare of the sun. He held his breath. No matter where she was, she always seemed comfortable in her skin. Even now, after they'd been apart for three years, it felt as if he'd never left.

Pounding reverberated through the room. He slid his gaze to the door.

"Amelia. Open this goddamn door!"

Joshua glanced at Amelia. Her shoulders went to her ears and her back ramrod straight. She seemed to shrink in on herself, and since he didn't recognize the voice, he'd treat the newcomer as an enemy. Actually, anyone demanding entrance in that manner was certainly an enemy.

He jerked on pants, crossed the room, and laid a gentle hand on her shoulder. "I've got this."

"I should put on a robe," she muttered.

"Why? Do you intend to leave the room?"

"I...no."

"Then enjoy the sun." Joshua stalked to the door, snatched it open a few inches, and moved in front of the gap. He looked at the man on the threshold, up and down. "You've got two seconds to state your business."

There was something familiar about the man's heavily tanned features, especially the way his dark brown eyes widened, then narrowed while his thin lips pursed. "What have you done with Amelia?"

"She's just fine. Was that all you wanted? Good. Be on your way." Joshua moved to slam the door, but the other man planted a palm on the wood. "What?"

Footsteps pounding in the hall distracted Joshua. The other man turned to see and let out a curse. "I'm sorry, Joshua. He got past me. The cops are here."

"Just because your brother is dead, doesn't mean you run this house," the man sneered.

"Actually it does. You may run things for my parents, but you don't run *this* house," Gage told him. "Remember. You can be replaced."

"You will do no such thing," the man huffed.

Joshua inwardly smiled at the way the other paled—his throat convulsed. The man wanted to say more, but Gage cut him off. "Actually your services are no longer required. If you leave quickly and quietly, I'll make sure you get a decent reference. If not..." Gage let the statement hang.

The man clenched his fists, hatred blazing in his eyes as he took a menacing step toward Gage. Joshua made a small noise and the man stilled.

"Will that be a problem?" Gage asked pleasantly.

"No," the man said tightly and walked away.

Joshua waited until the other man was out of sight before speaking. "You did good, kid, but I think you've made an enemy."

"I never liked him. The police are downstairs waiting for Amelia." Concern now shadowed his features. "Is she all right?"

"Sore."

He nodded, as if expecting the answer. "I'm really sorry I wasn't there for her last night."

"Don't worry about it. Let them know we'll be down soon."

Gage nodded as Joshua closed the door.

"Amelia. The police are waiting to question you."

She swung around to face him. "My entire family will be there. I can do this by myself."

"You've done enough things by yourself. I'm not leaving your side."

Her lips quirked upward at the corners before they drooped again. "My family will be there."

He cupped her cheek. "From this moment on, I'm not leaving your side. If you have a problem with that, say so now." He drifted his gaze over her face. Her left cheek was swollen, and her bottom lip bore a deep split from her ordeal. "Get dressed. We'll do this together."

Voices drifted to them as they entered the hall. Whether she knew it or not, Amelia clutched his arm in a viselike grip. Joshua covered her hand with his. "Regardless of what happens, I will keep you safe."

She nodded.

"And we'll find out what happened."

She shook her head.

He paused and turned her to face him. "You don't want to know why this happened?"

Something akin to fear skittered across her face. "I don't want to bury you again."

"I'm not going anywhere. I'm a civilian now, Lia. No more assignments." He tucked her hand in the crook of his arm. "Now, let's go face the authorities."

When they entered the room, all conversation ceased, and the grip on his arm tightened. Kiska emitted a low growl. "Relax. Lia." Joshua eyed his former in-laws with practiced indifference.

Chad Tyler, an associate at Amelia's law firm, stood in front of the wet bar. He shot a glare in his direction before he continued pouring an amber liquid into a rocks glass. The man had gained weight since Joshua had last seen him, and his facial features had softened from too much liquor and rich food.

Joshua narrowed his gaze. *Is that a dark spot across Chad's cheek?*

Chad raised the glass to his lips. The pinky and ring fingers were taped together. Could this man have been one of Amelia's attackers? Chad was the right height and weight. *But what would be his motive?*

Interesting how the man projected the air of being in charge, but one glare at Amelia and Joshua knew it was all an act. He would need to dig a little deeper on Chad.

Joshua traded glances with the man who'd demanded entry. With a steno pad balanced on one pinstripe clad knee, he placed him, but couldn't recall his name. Was the man deliberately flaunting his disregard of his dismissal or was this a final act of service?

Gage walked in, followed by two men and a woman. The woman was slick and polished, wearing a good summer weight suit tailored to accentuate her assets. This was confirmed by the younger of the two men sending her appreciative looks. Joshua thought the woman resembled a spider; she had short torso, and long thin arms and legs.

Gage scowled at the secretary and the other interlopers but said nothing as he took a chair near the door.

The officers now stood in the center of the room, their shiny polished shoes at odds with their more casual clothing. The older man, graying at the temples of his receding hairline, bore a no-nonsense expression, as if he'd seen too many problems regarding this family.

The other officer, his dark brown hair stood in gelled spikes, held contempt in his gaze as he looked at Amelia and the bruises. Joshua shifted beside her, putting his body between her and the others.

He led Amelia to a high back, overstuffed chair. It was the only chair that wasn't near a window, and it faced the hallway where he would have the perfect view of those coming in and out of the room.

"Two officers are standing. Your sister, Leigh, is here, and I believe Chad Tyler from your firm is here as well."

Shaking her head, she opened her mouth to say something but then promptly closed it.

"And that secretary Gage just fired." This was said just loud enough for the man to hear. Heat colored his cheeks.

She nodded as she sat; the dog laid at her feet while Joshua perched on the arm. He caught Gage's attention. The younger man nodded and shifted his attention to the hall beyond, almost as if he'd done this before. Joshua would have to ask him.

"Glad you could join us Mrs. Bedford," said the taller of the pair. "I'm Sergeant Falls and my partner Potter. First, allow me to extend my condolences on your recent loss."

Amelia inclined her head. "Thank you."

"We were unable to gather any information from you last night about the attack. As your companion said, you were too upset at the time. Is there anything you can tell us now?"

A ripple of tension scurried through the room as everyone seemed to wait for her answer.

"They were strong. One had really bad body odor. He attacked me first. I think I broke the fingers on his left hand and possibly his nose. Kiska may have gotten a piece of him too." She twisted her fingers in her lap.

Joshua rested a hand on her shoulder before kneading the tight muscles in her neck. Her hands stilled, and she released a barely audible exhale.

"And the other man?" Falls prompted.

Amelia was silent a moment, worrying her bottom lip. Though, she should've been the center of attention, all eyes were focused on him. Tension was almost as palpable as the chair he sat on. Joshua met each hostile glare with arrogance. He didn't give a damn what these people thought of him, and he cared even less now. Someone in this room went to a lot of trouble to hurt Amelia, and he would find out who.

"Knocked me to the ground and held something sharp to my throat." She stroked her neck below the chin. A long thin scratch was there. "He told me to call off my dog or else." She managed a wry smile. "I told him I couldn't breathe. When he shifted, I screamed again. Then someone knocked him off me." She leaned forward in her chair. "Carter. Carter was injured too. Is he all right?"

"Who's Carter?" This was from Potter.

"Her driver," Gage spoke up. "He's been with us for years."

"Why is she so concerned about the help? I'll never understand. He can be replaced for not doing his job," Leigh muttered.

"He is a person, Leigh, and deserves respect," Amelia admonished. "You don't need to be here for this." She peered at each person in the room. The gesture so uncanny when everyone knew she couldn't see them. "None of you need to be here except Gage and Joshua."

Joshua bit the inside of his cheek to keep from smiling, even as Gage snorted a laugh. She still had her morals.

"We spoke with him last night. They should release him sometime today," Falls said.

"What were you doing walking through the gardens at that time of night?" This was from Potter, his tone more antagonistic.

She tensed beneath Joshua's hand, but he didn't let go. Instead, he continued to massage her shoulders.

"I needed to clear my head after the repast. The gardens always bring me a measure of peace. Besides, I wasn't by myself."

"You're blind, yet you say you broke fingers and a nose?"

"Potter." A warning note clung to his partner's voice.

Amelia lifted her chin. "Detective Potter, I am blind, but that doesn't mean I'm helpless. Let me see. You're married, yet you have no problem sleeping around. There are three distinct perfumes on your clothing. I smell garlic as well, and the peppermint gum you keep cracking isn't doing much to hide the fact you had a drink just before you arrived here."

Joshua watched the man's eyes narrow, and his face redden. "I think she's proven her point."

"You told her to say those things," Potter sputtered.

Kiska raised her head and growled. "Watch your tone, Detective. Kiska is more than just Amelia's guide. She's also her protector," Joshua warned. "And if you're not afraid of the dog, try me next." He stood, a quiet calm contradicting the menace in his words.

Potter stepped closer. "Are you threatening an officer?"

Joshua looked him up and down. "Amelia, honey. You're absolutely correct. There is a bit a whiskey on his breath." He glanced over the man's shoulder to Falls. "Maybe you should get your partner and detox him. I'd hate for the man to have an accident."

"Potter. Back off," Falls ordered.

Cool fingers wrapped around his wrist. Joshua didn't need to glance down to know Amelia wanted him to stand down. That wasn't an option. No one, and that included some half-drunk detective, was going to insult Amelia.

Falls grabbed Potter by the arm. "Back off! Wait for me in the car."

"You're going to let this..."

"Outside. Now!"

With one last scathing glare, Potter stomped from the room.

"You always do this when people try to help," snapped Leigh as she hurried after the man.

"My apologies, Mr. Hastings. I'll deal with my partner later."

"Do that. The next time he insults Amelia, I won't be so polite."

Falls nodded. "From the injuries you've described, Mrs. Bedford, it shouldn't be too hard to find these men. Is there anything else you remember? Their voices? Maybe their clothing?"

"The man who spoke, he had a smoker's voice, but I really can't be sure. He whispered a lot. As far as clothing...

cotton shirts, nylon pants. They made swishy sounds when they moved."

"Swishy?" Chad snorted. "Really, Amelia. You come out better saying nothing at all."

Amelia smiled politely. "And who called you, Chad? I don't believe you're anywhere on my emergency contact. As a matter of fact, you're not even welcome in my home. Or did you forget that part of the settlement?"

"I, uh, thought you would need representation. Just in case."

"I'd be a fool before I allow you to represent me. It's one thing not to trust a client, it's another when I know I can't trust the lawyer." It was said pleasantly enough, but the cutting edge was there. "I do believe Leigh left. You might want to find her and represent her interests. She's less discerning than I."

Chad had now turned an angry red, his mouth opening and closing as he fought for something to say.

"I have a partial plate number." Joshua spoke before the other man could. If he was mistaken, a collective gasp went through the room. Interesting. He pulled a slip of paper from his pocket. "That should get you started."

"Did you see either attacker, Mr. Hastings?"

"They wore masks," he said as he eyed Chad, not surprised to see small beads of perspiration above Chad's lip.

Falls nodded. "Thanks. I'll gather this information and get back to you."

Joshua inclined his head. "Please do. I'd like to stay in the loop as much as possible with this." He extracted a card from his pocket. "My contact information."

"Very well."

The two men shook hands. Then Falls left.

The quick staccato of high heels on marble preceded Leigh. Gage swiped a hand down his face. "In-laws are so irritating."

"Shut up, you horrid little boy."

Gage feigned hurt. "Wow. Such big words from an aging debutante." He cupped a hand to his ear. "What's that? I believe the silicone in your face is cracking. It's not supposed to bend that way."

She jabbed a red lacquered nail at him. "I'll deal with you later." She whirled on Joshua. "Back from the dead I see."

Chad narrowed his eyes. "This is the irritant you wanted me to see?" he asked.

Gage stepped forward, and Joshua waved him off. He kept his body between the three unwanted guests and Amelia.

"Just so we're clear. Things will change around here. Whatever game you're running on Amelia, ends now. I will find out which one of you did this to us, and when I do, you'll pay for every tear she's shed."

Chapter Eight

The slide of curtain hooks grated on Victor's already overwrought senses. He peeled one sandpaper covered eye open and winced at the bright sunlight. He allowed the lid to close, and tiny shards of pain bombarded his brain. "Go away," he said with a moan. "You're ruining a smashing hangover."

"Hastings is back." The man stomped through the room.

Each thud reverberated through his skull like a mallet to a metal drum. "Who the fuck is that, and why should I care?" Victor tossed an arm over his eyes and flopped onto his back. As long as he focused on his hangover, he didn't have to feel the overwhelming grief and guilt gnawing at his gut every day. The alcohol wouldn't bring Gareth back, but it would certainly dull the ache of despair.

The sheet was unceremoniously yanked from his body. Victor lowered his arm just enough to offer the scowling man an off-centered smile. "I didn't think you swung that way, mate, but if you're game, so am I."

"I just had to sit through that smug little bitch stripping me raw in front of a bunch of people once again. It was bad enough she discovered me stealing, but she's done humiliating me." The man turned away in disgust. "I have no idea what Gareth saw in you, but you're a disgrace to his memory. Get cleaned up."

"You're banging her sister, mate. What more do you want from me?"

"I want what should be mine!" he snapped. "I brought that copyright case to her. And did I get the credit? No. She fires me. Now get up!"

"I did everything you asked, and he's still dead." Victor rolled out of bed with a groan. He cradled his pounding skull in his hands. "I wished I'd died with him."

"That can be arranged."

Victor twisted his head. "Go away. I can't deal with you right now."

"Well you're going to deal. Hastings is back."

"Who is Hastings?"

"Amelia's first husband."

Victor scrubbed his hand across his face, then his jaw dropped. "No. I thought…"

A sneer twisted the other man's lips. "It would be a shame to waste that nice plot Amelia picked out for him, don't you think? This time she can join him."

Mr. VIP studied the wide entryway and the brilliant chandelier hanging from the high vaulted ceiling. She married into money. Had his cheating ex-wife not robbed him, he could've given her a house like this. On the other hand, he'd liked Gareth Bedford, the attorney who'd handled not just the dissolution of his business, but his divorce too. Gareth had even offered to invest in his company, but there was no point. Mr. VIP was too far in the red for anyone to help, even with Gareth's generous offer.

But Gareth was gone and so would Amelia.

He carefully clutched a small, covered basket in two hands. The lid was tied in place, held down with a bungee cord. He smiled at the thin man wearing a pinstriped slacks and black dress shirt.

"You are here to see Mrs. Bedford," Dawson intoned.

Mr. VIP smirked. "No need to put on airs. I know you don't like Amelia." His smile widened. "I don't like her much either."

He nearly laughed at the surprise on the other man's face.

"I see."

"Now that we have that out the way...I could use your assistance."

A wary gleam edged Dawson's eyes. "I am no longer employed by this family after today." He sniffed.

"Even more reason for your assistance." Mr. VIP held out the basket. "I'd like to place this in Amelia's room."

"Her suite of rooms are locked. Not even I can enter without her permission."

"Let me worry about the logistics of entering her rooms. I just need to know I won't be caught while I'm leaving my little gift."

Understanding dawned and Dawson grinned. "Of course. Follow me."

Amelia touched a tentative tongue to the inside of her cheek. She winced. Sore but at least there were no loose teeth. She'd been very lucky not to be injured more than what she already was. *If Joshua hadn't been there...*

Footsteps. She tilted her head and listened. More than one pair sounded on the wood floor. A knock preceded as her office door opened.

"Mrs. Bedford." Dawson couldn't quite mask the note of derision in his voice.

"Yes, Dawson," she returned coolly.

"Mr. VIP is here to see you."

"Thank you." Amelia stood, intending to greet her guest.

"No. Don't get up," Mr. VIP said.

The door clicked signaling they were alone.

"Could I get you something to drink?" Amelia asked, turning to the small fridge nestled in the credenza behind her desk.

"No, thank you." A chair scraped, and the springs squeaked as he sat. "I stopped by to thank you and offer my condolences."

Amelia swallowed hard. "Thank you."

"Your husband was very nice to me when he handled my affairs. I'm very sorry to see him go."

She nodded, not trusting her voice.

"I heard you were attacked last night."

Self-consciously, she touched her bruised and swollen cheek. "You should see the other guy," she replied lightly.

He chuckled. "Serves them right for picking a fight with you." He paused. "Well, I'm glad you're okay, and if you need to talk, just give me a call." The chair scraped.

Amelia stood as well. She rounded the desk, stopping just outside his personal bubble. "Are you okay?" She focused in his general direction. "You don't sound like your usual self."

"This hasn't been easy. Losing everything I love at one time." He managed a self-deprecating laugh. "But you know what that's like."

"I do," she murmured. "It takes a long time to recover. If a person can recover at all."

He patted her hand. "Was that Joshua I saw at the repast?"

"Yes."

"It's good you get a second chance." The swish of clothes indicated he moved away. "I'll show myself out."

Before she could say anything else, the door closed. Amelia stood there for a moment. She wasn't sure, but Mr. VIP didn't sound right. With a sigh, she left her office. Hopefully some Pilates will clear her mind and ease some of the soreness in her body.

She mounted the steps to the second floor, Kiska keeping pace. A slow smile creased her lips as she neared the top. Joshua was alive.

Joshua stared at the spreadsheets littering the surface of the oversized mahogany desk. Three more stacks were waiting for his scrutiny. He compared the totals to the tax statements in his hand. Something was definitely off with the numbers.

He set the papers aside and sat down at the computer. Movement captured the corner of his eye and dragged his attention in that direction. Amelia stood, her front leg bent at a ninety-degree angle while her back leg stretched behind her. She stretched her arms straight out perpendicular to the floor, exhaled, and slowly brought her palms together over her head. She leaned back, her round breasts thrusting toward the sun in greeting as she completed the warrior's pose. She repeated the movement several times before she brought her feet together and stood upright.

Mesmerized, he absently shifted his sudden arousal. It wasn't just her exercising. She was doing it in the nude. Amelia did everything in the nude when she was in her suite. That was one of the things that had attracted him to her when he had met her at a club demo years ago.

He was a guest of one of the members. As soon as the demo ended, he garnered an introduction. The fact she hadn't been flustered in his presence at her nudity, the instant attraction only made him want to know her better.

She transitioned into balancing on one leg. She leaned forward, sticking her leg out behind her while she leaned forward, her arms in front of her. Her body was now in the shape of a T. Work aside, he had to know if she still retained the control he taught her. He grabbed the little keyboard duster as he stood and with deliberate care approached her.

"Don't move," he murmured. A visible tremor and a quick inhale were the only indicators she'd heard him. Starting with the outstretched leg, he skimmed the duster over her toes, up her instep, and finally her calf.

A soft sigh filled the air. She trembled but maintained her pose.

"Very good." He stroked the curve of her derriere, admiring the firmness. He bent and placed a kiss at the base of her spine. "Switch legs."

She wobbled a tad as she lowered her leg, bent at the knees for a quick stretch, then resumed the pose on her other limb. He repeated his caress, mindful of her bruises as he traveled up her leg, teasing the curve of her behind.

The faint scent of her arousal perfumed the air as he lingered, drawing a breathy whimper from her body. His groin tightened. Mere hours and it was if they'd never been apart.

"What's next, Lia?" He swirled the duster up her spine.

"Child's pose." She lowered her leg, shifting until her feet were together, bent at the waist, and lowered her body in a graceful manner. She rested a moment on her knees, her buttocks touching her heels.

Joshua stood in front of her and stroked her face. Her eyes fluttered closed, and her lips parted. Stealing the ripeness of her mouth would be too easy. She was just too damn willing, just too easy to fall back into their same old routine.

Abruptly, he stepped away. Disappointment skittered across her face. "Continue."

She nodded, lowered her head, and moved until her breasts touched her knees, then drew her arms on either side of her. Her forehead rested on the mat. Joshua watched the rise and fall of her back.

In another time and place, he'd swirl a silk scarf, or flogger, or a hairbrush. A smile tugged at his lips; she seemed to like the drag of fine sandpaper across her skin. Or the lighter touch of a cotton ball. But it wasn't just that, her skin was temptation. He wanted to stroke her, imprint the texture of her flesh into his memory, sample the delicate flavor that was all her and indulge his senses with each breathy moan.

Before he could stop himself, he leaned over, grabbed a handful of her hair, and brought it to his nose. He inhaled, taking the sweet scent of brown sugar deep into his lungs. Too many nights he dreamed about the way she smelled, the way she felt and often thought of ways to make her pay for what she'd done.

Lia held perfectly still, measuring each breath as it entered, then exited her lungs. She'd missed Joshua's touch so much, and the slight roughness of his fingers grazing her skin left her edgy and unfulfilled. Gareth had been good about holding or cuddling her throughout the day. Even when they played, there was a connection. But never like what she shared with Joshua.

Joshua always seemed to know what she really needed before she voiced it. Like when they were downstairs, simply rubbing her shoulders to ease her anxiety. Or earlier, when she was nearly panicking, he still offered comfort. And even now, combing his fingers through her hair, she wanted to stay in this pose forever.

Tears burned behind her lids. She didn't expect an immediate reconnect. But despite his caresses, she sensed an underlying anger directed toward her. She swallowed the lump in her throat. Had she known he wasn't dead, she'd have used every means at her disposal to find him. She wouldn't have left him behind.

Her hair fell against her back, and she felt him move away. She inhaled a stuttered breath and waited for his next order. Nothing. Seconds ticked into minutes. Nothing. Clothing rustled, followed by his footsteps walking away from her. Disappointment licked at her heart.

"You may finish and go about your day."

The cold dismissal was a slap. After everything he'd done, the rejection cut deep. She unfolded from her pose and stretched out on her back. A few deep breaths would not return her calm or dispel the ache welling inside. Carefully, she made it to her feet, rolled her mat, and placed it back into the closet. She turned to enter the bathroom.

"Lia?"

The commanding note in his voice held her captive. She allowed the way he said her name to wash over her, soothing her jangled nerves. "Yes," she replied.

"Do not masturbate in the shower."

Her jaw dropped. After everything, that's all he had to say? "You don't give me orders anymore." A blur of color rushed before her eyes. She stumbled back, the coolness of the wall bringing her up short.

"No?" His breath was moist on her face. "You still wear my collar."

She gritted her teeth and raised her chin in defiance. The weight of her necklace eased around her throat. How had he lifted it without touching her skin?

"Are you ready to take this off?"

Panic wiggled through her. She didn't want to lose that connection, but she would if it means proving her point.

"If you feel I have violated what this represents," she tapped the chain, "then by all means, take it. When I thought you were dead, I didn't know if I would survive the grief. Knowing you're alive, I may not survive your fury. Had I known you were alive, I'd have spared no expense in finding you."

The chain tightened at her throat. For several heartbeats, she believed he'd just snatch it away.

He pressed into her, his hair tickling her cheek as his lips found hers.

He wrapped her in sensation. The smoothness of his shirt against her skin, the roughness of his hands as he explored her body. She was lost in texture and the masculine taste of him.

She was lifted, and she wrapped her legs around his waist, the evidence of his arousal nestled at her core. His trousers were the only barrier. He settled her in the bed, and there were no more barriers.

She ran her hands over his chiseled muscles. Everything about him was hard and lean. Before she could go farther, he captured her wrists in one hand and held them above her head.

"Tell me you're ready for me?" he demanded.

She arched toward him. "Yes." No man had taken her since the last time they we're together. No amount of vibrators or dildos would ever take the place of the flesh and blood of this man stroking her now.

"I can't be gentle, Lia. Not right now."

"I don't want gentle."

He was inside her before she finished the sentence. It had been so long and yet like they'd never been apart.

Joshua stroked deep, not giving her time to change her mind or his. Three years was too long to go without his Lia. And God, she was so tight and wet. He shifted her legs until they rested on his shoulders, leaned forward and once more pinned her hands to the bed.

Her first orgasm burst through her, surprising them both. Her keening cry fueled his lust for more.

It wasn't sex. It wasn't love. He claimed her, branding her in a way so intimate their souls rejoiced at their joining.

He left her wrist to grasp her hips and pounded into her pliant depths. When she climaxed again, he followed her over the cliff, roaring his release.

He collapsed over her. She held him close, stroking his back with gentle, reverent fingers. She pressed a kiss to his shoulder. He shifted, easing his weight from her body.

"Did I hurt you?" He lightly ran his hands over her, checking to make sure he hadn't aggravated any of her injuries with his hastiness.

She shook her head.

He rested his forehead on hers. "Lia, I never stopped loving you."

Tears slipped down her cheeks. "I love you so much, Joshua. Please don't leave me again."

He kissed her tears away. "I won't. He lifted her from the bed. "C'mon. Let's shower together."

He left her in the shower. Joshua quickly dried off and dressed in jeans, a tee, and tossed on a button-up. He combed his damp tresses and secured it with a leather tie at the nape of his neck. He donned his holster and weapon before padding to the table, to the papers there.

He stared at the surface without seeing anything. His blood and body still hummed from loving. He hadn't planned on taking her, but she challenged him and quite frankly called his bluff. He could no more snatch his collar from her than cut off his own arm. She had believed he was dead while someone else made him believed she'd discarded him like trash.

He expelled a breath and stared at the ceiling. This was more complicated than he realized. The attraction was still there, more potent than ever. Even now, with the faint thunder of the shower seeping through the closed door, he wanted to join her.

He forced his attention to the paperwork in front of him. Something in all these numbers was bothering him. His phone jittered on the desk. He swept a finger across the display and lifted the device to his ear. "Hastings."

"The vehicle belongs to Bedford Industries," the caller said without preamble.

"No surprise there."

"It was reported stolen yesterday morning," he continued.

"That's convenient."

"It is. The police have it in their impound lot now. Although, I called in a favor, and we were able to get a look inside the vehicle but not touch anything."

He leaned back in the chair. "Find anything interesting?"

"A photo of Amelia. Looks like this crew didn't know what the widow Bedford looked like," Paper rattled through the line. "She's an attractive woman."

Jealousy rolled in his gut. "She is."

"No worries from me, Joshua. I've done my homework. I know she's your ex, and she's off limits."

"You'd do well to keep that in mind. Also, I need you to give me everything on a Detective Potter."

"What's up?"

"He took an instant dislike to Amelia."

"Not the usual good cop/bad cop routine?"

Hinges squeaked, and Joshua glanced over his shoulder. "No. Get that info to me as soon as possible."

"Will do."

Joshua hung up the phone and turned in his chair. Amelia emerged from the bathroom, a large fluffy towel winding her body. Droplets of water dotted her skin, and he longed to lick them away. He stifled a groan as she crossed the room to a heavy armoire. Kiska jumped to her feet, trotted to where Amelia stood, and pushed against her knees.

"Kiska. Stop." Amelia reached down and scratched the dog's ears. "I need to get dressed, love." When she aimed for the knob again, the animal growled and snapped at her hand. "What has gotten into you?"

Joshua stood. "Amelia."

"Did you put my dog up to this?" she demanded. "Seriously. Now I can't even get dressed?"

"Why would she normally growl at you?" He kept his voice even as he approached.

She straightened, grabbing her towel. "If there's something that will hurt me or I'm headed in the wrong direction." She reached for the armoire again. This time the dog nudged her, nearly knocking her over. Josh grabbed her by the elbow to steady her. "Fine. I'll stay naked."

Amusement tugged at Joshua's lips. As much as he enjoyed seeing Amelia walk around sans clothing, he knew not everyone shared his perspective. "Why don't I take a look. Grab Kiska and go over by the desk."

He waited until she crossed the room before approaching the furniture. For one moment, he thought there could be a bomb attached to the door, and he pressed his ear to the wood. Just a hiss and a faint rattle. *Odd*.

He stepped beside the wardrobe, grabbed the knob, and yanked open the door.

An object darted out, the sound unmistakable as it reared its head and hissed at him. Joshua jumped back. "Amelia. On the bed. Now!" From the corner of his eye, he watched her move. Both dog and woman climbed onto the mattress.

"What is it?"

"Rattlesnake."

"Ohmygosh."

Indeed. With deliberate steps, he moved backward. The snake shot forward. Joshua jerked his firearm from its holster and fired. Amelia screamed behind him. He waved a hand, clearing the smoke from his face.

The snake lay dead.

Chapter Nine

"Joshua. Joshua!" Amelia clutched the dog's collar as she knelt on the bed. Heart lodged in her throat, she listened for any type of movement. The sudden explosion of gunfire left her blood cold, and if he didn't answer her... "Please." She moved toward the edge of the bed, and Kiska barked.

A hand closed over the back of her neck. "I'm here." Fingers threaded through her hair, before her head was tilted back. Lips moved over hers. She moaned, tangling her fingers in his shirt.

Footsteps pounded. A loud thud filled the silence. "Amelia! Joshua! What's going on?" Gage pounded on the door. "Dammit. Let me in."

Locks clicked, and the door flew open. Gage stopped at the threshold. Behind him were Chad and Leigh.

"What the hell is going on in here?"

Joshua released her in slow degrees. "Someone placed a rattlesnake in Amelia's wardrobe. I killed it."

Kiska growled.

"You know I don't like that damn dog, Amelia. Keep hold of her," Leigh said.

"The feeling is mutual, Leigh."

Leigh huffed. "I don't see why you keep that nasty fleabag anyway," she muttered.

"At least she does what she's told," Gage retorted.

"Did I hear a gunshot?" This was from Chad.

"I just said I killed the snake." His words brushed her cheek as silk slid over her shoulders. "Your robe," he murmured into her ear.

She threaded her arms through the sleeves, then grabbed his hand before he could move away. "Are you sure you're okay?" He lifted her hand and placed it on his cheek. Aside from the fine hairs of his beard, his jaw was tight, but he nodded. A sigh eased past her lips. "And the snake?"

"Dealt with but I want you to stay put until I check everything. Then I'm taking you out of here."

She clutched him. "You can't. We can't leave Gage here alone."

"Why are they still here?" Joshua asked pleasantly.

"They were leaving when we all heard the gunshot," Gage answered.

"And how did you get in?" Joshua stepped toward Gage.

Gage swallowed hard. "Gar-Gareth gave me an override. In case of an emergency. I thought this was an emergency."

He held Gage's eyes. "So Doughboy and Gold Digger are only here because Gareth is dead, and they think they can run roughshod over you."

"That about sums it up."

"Let's remedy that right now."

"You can't throw us out," Chad sputtered.

"She's my sister, and she's grieving," Leigh tried.

Joshua grabbed each by an arm and forced them to the door. "If either of you are still on the premises within five minutes I will have you arrested for trespassing. If you return, I'll file charges for stalking Gage."

"Yes, sir?"

"Please escort these people out." He gave them both a slight shove, then reached into his pocket. He handed Gage a card. "Call this number. Tell them you need security for the estate. Give them my name, and someone should be here within thirty minutes."

"Will do."

Joshua closed and locked the door on the protests and yells as Gage followed his instructions.

Behind him, the bed creaked.

"Don't move from the bed, Lia."

She huffed, and he fought back a chuckle. She was just as impatient as ever. He moved around the room, scooped the dead snake into a pillowcase, and set it into a nearby trashcan. Maybe he could find out who purchased it. Something like that had to have been flown in, and there had to be a record.

"I don't want to leave my home, Joshua. Will they come back?"

Joshua swung around and briefly stared at her. Worry creased her brow, and she sucked her bottom lip between her teeth. Her fingers were twined in the dog's fur. He blew out a breath. He could give her this. "I have a security firm. Gage is calling them, and they will be here to provide protection until the threat is vanquished."

"And they'll protect Gage as well?" She sat on the edge of the bed, her feet dangling.

"Their priority is you."

She lifted her chin. "Gage is my brother now. You make sure he stays alive, or you will not get my cooperation."

"And what will you do?" Amusement lit his tone.

"Call in someone who will do as I ask."

He dragged a finger down her collarbone, hooking it in the vee of the robe. He gave a little tug, exposing her cleavage.

She slapped his hand away from the garment. "You think someone is trying to kill me. Someone did kill Gareth. What's to stop them from getting to Gage?"

"Someone is. One of your relatives is an obvious choice. Gareth's death made you and Gage extremely wealthy."

"If it's about the money, they can have it. I never wanted it to begin with." She got up and started to pace. Kiska jumped off the bed, shadowing her steps. "But there's that stupid clause preventing me from just giving it away."

He smiled. This was a familiar lament. Amelia never wanted to be rich, believing the money was more trouble than it was worth. "Well, you seem to do very well with your inheritance."

"And now someone is trying to kill me for it."

"You don't sound surprised."

"Can I tell you something and you not freak out?"

Joshua studied her a moment. Her breathing had picked up, and she was twisting her fingers in the folds of her robe. He gently plucked her hand and held it between his. "What is it?"

"I think Gareth was killed because of something Victor was doing."

"What makes you say that?"

She hesitated, worrying her lip.

"Lia?"

"I feel like I'm gossiping."

"You live here with them. You pick up on nuances most of us don't. People tend to speak around you because you're blind. Anything you tell me will help find who killed Gareth, and who is trying to kill you."

"I think Victor was gambling again," she finally relented. "I don't know what made this time different. All I know is Gareth was very protective of me in the days before he died. Well weeks. Especially after someone tried to hit me with a car."

"When did that happen?" he snapped out the question.

She hunched her shoulders at the tone.

Joshua breathed in deep. "I'm sorry. When?"

"I'd have to check my calendar. It was our last council meeting."

"You still go to those?" The smile was evident in his voice.

"Absolutely. They're a great bunch of people."

"When's the next meeting?"

"They postponed it because of the funeral."

Joshua cupped her cheek. "I'm sorry about Gareth."

She kissed his palm. "I am too."

Dressed in loose fitting capris and an oversized shirt, Amelia sat in her home office, reading through a transcript from a recent interview she'd done with a client. This was one of the last cases she'd discussed with Gareth as he enjoyed finding holes before closing them up into trust funds.

Lightly, her fingertips skimmed the braille on the stiff paper.

Though she still utilized the classic Perkins Brailler, technology had advanced to a braille printer. Someone could type as a sighted person, and the printer would spit out the text in braille. No muss. No fuss. She had one here, including the office at the firm.

She paused on a paragraph; a frown creased her lips. This wasn't right. She set the page aside to find the same document on the computer, using the accessibility feature to read the same passage.

A knock sounded on the door. Kiska emitted a quick woof.

"Come in," she called.

"I can come back if you're busy," Gage offered.

"I'm never too busy for you. What's up?"

"Maybe I should ask you the same question. You're frowning."

"The documents aren't the same. Either my assistant changed after she printed these for me," she indicated to the pages on the desk, "or someone else changed them and didn't give me updated copies." She shook her head. "I'm sorry."

"It's okay. You're trying to stay busy."

"And you're hovering."

He chuckled. "I'm worried, Amelia. I can't do what Gareth did. He knew how to stand up to our parents and your family. He knew how to protect us, and I'm already failing."

Amelia stood, came around the desk, and sat next to him. She covered his hand with hers. "You're not failing," she assured him. "A good sign of courage is knowing when to ask for help. Gareth asked for help."

"He did?"

"I don't know what's going on," she confessed. "Whatever it is, it's something that got Gareth killed. And I'm next on their list."

"Does this have anything to do with Victor and the attorney you fired? Leigh has been popping up more often than usual."

"It does seem to involve all of them, doesn't it?"

"You have your Joshua again."

A slow smile parted her lips. "Yes."

"He's scary."

She laughed. "To the wrong people I suppose."

Gage shifted in his chair, the rustle of fabric indicating his movement. "I did what he asked. There are people here. They're questioning the live-in staff."

Amelia sat back, mulling over the information. Had someone gotten to some of the staff? She shook her head. Anything was possible. "Have you spoken to Victor?"

"Last I checked, he was still sleep." He gripped Amelia's fingers. "If he had anything to do with my brother's death, I'll kill him."

Wisely, she said nothing. Gage was grieving as much if not more than she was. Some instinct warned her Victor was in the middle of this. If he hadn't been involved in the planning of Gareth's death, then she knew who arranged it. She sat up straight. Which meant he could be a target. She stood.

"What is it?"

"We need to find Joshua." She clicked her tongue. Kiska came alert with a jangle of tags and a vigorous shake. "C'mon, girl."

Chapter Ten

Dawson stared at the computer screen and scowled. This could not be happening again. There was too much at stake for this to happen now. He checked the page of his notebook, then what he'd typed on the screen.

He shoved the keyboard away in frustration and surged to his feet. "The passwords have been changed!"

Paper rattled and the other occupant in the room. Victor peered at him above his newspaper, then returned to whatever had captured his attention. "And I should care about this why?"

Such insolence. He was not going to let this impudent pup stand in the way of all the careful plans he'd made. Dawson stomped across the marble floor, snatched the newspaper, and flung it across the room. "You should care since everything I have arranged is about to blow up in your face. No passwords mean no money."

"Gareth is dead! Who gives a fuck about the money?" Victor surged to his feet. It was then that Dawson read grief, stark and palatable on the man's face. Hovering just below the surface was anger. He'd pushed too hard, and the tentative hold he'd had on Victor was quickly unraveling.

Victor shoved him back. "I did everything you asked, and he's still dead. Besides, I heard what happened last night. Did you really think a rattlesnake in Amelia's armoire would help? And she knows her husband is alive." He shook his head. "He probably changed the passwords. He was always protective of her."

He jerked Victor up by the front of his shirt. "That's the point. You need to get close to Amelia."

Victor snatched away, stumbling into a nearby table. The expensive vase seated on the surface wobbled, then crashed onto the floor. He straightened his clothes. "I'm done. Whatever else you need, do it yourself."

"That arrogant little punk fired me. I'm not even supposed to be on the premises. You have to do this."

Victor stared at him. "Gareth is dead."

The temper Dawson held in check boiled to the surface as he stalked toward Victor. "You owe me."

Victor stared at him dispassionately. "My debt was paid when Gareth died. Your plan failed. You had access to her entire fortune; you should've taken it then. Find another pansy to do your dirty work."

"I've invested too much time for you to back out now."

The other man's eyes widened. "Back off, Dawson."

"You and no one else will keep me from getting what is rightfully mine."

Victor stumbled backward. Dawson pounced, knocking the smaller man to the floor. Glass shattered as both men careened into a table and fell to the floor. Dawson pressed his advantage, wrapping his hands around Victor's windpipe and squeezing for all he was worth.

Victor bucked and thrashed beneath him, but Dawson leaned his weight against him. Desperate fingernails clawed at the backs of his hands as Victor's eyes bulged. Dawson couldn't ignore the wiggle of delight that flickered down his spine. Watching the light fade from someone's eyes was a rush he couldn't ignore. He'd recorded the explosion and viewed the tape several times. The moment before Gareth met his demise was priceless. His only regret was not actually witnessing the light fading. But that moment of shock, when he opened that one special little box, was priceless.

His grip loosened as he recalled the flash. Pain exploded in his skull. Dawson fell to the side, clutching his head. He pulled his hand away. Blood and moisture coated his palm. With his other hand, he patted the floor next to him.

"What the... You tried to kill me?" Victor stood over the man, gasping. "Have you lost your mind?"

Dawson lay there, temper smoldering. He waited for his moment. When Victor leaned down, he moved. Surprise shown on the other man's face, and Dawson bared his teeth in a sneer. Victor stumbled back, clutching his abdomen, bright red seeping between his fingers and staining his shirt.

"You won't get away with this," he murmured.

"Don't worry. I already have."

"Are you going to tell me what you discovered?" Gage asked as he kept pace with Amelia.

"Something Joshua said. Nothing big. I think that's what's been bothering me. It's been a lot of little things. Victor kept saying it was his fault, but what could've been his fault?"

They traversed the cool tiled floors, giving way to a plush strip of carpet. This was the beginning of the stairs.

Kiska stepped down one riser. Amelia followed, grasping the handrail as an additional guide. Gage hurried down, waiting for her at the bottom.

Footsteps were muted on another strip of carpet before they clicked their way across the foyer. "I'm not sure where he would be."

"Probably the family room," she suggested. "At least, that's where Gareth conducted all of his business."

The low murmur of a deep baritone drifted to her ears. She followed the sound as she carefully navigated through another hall and set of doors.

A chime split the air. "I'll catch up. I need to take this call," Gage told her.

Amelia continued forward.

"What do you mean?" Joshua's words were clearer now, drifting out. "No. Say that again. Who's in the hospital?"

Amelia paused, her heart pounding in her chest. Had someone else been hurt? She inched forward, straining her ears for the other side of the conversation, but she could only hear Joshua's melodious tones.

"No. She and Kiska are safe." There was a pause. Amelia reached out a hand, her fingertips grazing smooth paneling. She was three doors away from the family room. "After this morning's incident, I wasn't taking any more chances."

She listened a moment, trying to determine where he was in the room. Kiska nudged the back of her knee, and Amelia moved to her left, allowing the dog to guide her.

Joshua's voice grew louder. "Were you able to get anything from her driver?"

Something hard and sharp jabbed her thigh, and she gasped as pain slid up and down her limb. She rubbed her palm over the spot on her leg while her other hand explored what she ran in to: a table. *Damn that hurt*. She limped forward. Someone must've moved the furniture and not told her. *I hate when they do that.*

"Bring him by. I'd like to speak with him." Joshua's voice was much louder. In fact, it sounded like he was right in front of her. A hand gripped her bicep. "Are you okay? No. I was speaking to Amelia. I think she ran into something." He paused. "Yes. Later this evening will be fine." A quiet click confirmed he'd ended the conversation. "Did you need something, Lia?"

"Do you know who moved the table? It's not supposed to be there."

"I'm sorry." Furniture scraped. "Where is it supposed to be? I think someone in security moved it so he could speak with the staff."

Amelia waited until the legs stopped scraping across the floor and said, "Have you spoken to Victor?"

"I've been trying to reach him."

"There's a cottage at the back of the estate. That's where he and Gareth lived."

"You're limping."

"It's nothing. I bumped into the table."

He grasped her hand and threaded it through the crook of his arm. "Come with me."

"Where are we going?" With his firm grasp on her hand, she had no choice but to follow.

"Back to your rooms. You're limping and in pain. I can't watch you any longer in such discomfort."

"It was just a table, Joshua," she protested.

"It's more than the table, Lia."

"But Gage and I needed to talk to you."

"It can wait."

"What's going on?" she demanded.

He led her down the hall, back through the set of doors, and to the strip of carpet before the stairs.

"But this is important." She mounted the steps.

"So are you and I've been woefully negligent."

She paused at the top step. "You've only been back for less than twenty-four hours. I don't expect us to pick up where we left off."

"Why not?" He crowded her until they made it to her bedroom.

Amelia unleashed and unharnessed the dog, then put them on a hook near the door. Kiska trotted off. A squeaky toy signaled Kiska had settled in.

"There's still plenty of stuff we need to discuss."

"Of course there is." He took her arm and led her across the room to another door.

She inhaled. Lemongrass and lavender permeated the air.

"I did some exploring while you were working." A scratch and fizz of a match preceded the scent of patouli. "Now strip."

She gasped. "What?"

He placed her hand on a smooth, padded surface. "You're in pain. You favor your ribs on one side, and you were limping before you ran into the table. Take off your clothes."

"Are we back to that again?"

A heavy sigh reached her ears.

"Joshua?"

"Lia. A massage will work wonders, and to do that, you need to take off your clothes." She could almost hear equal parts of exasperation and humor in his voice.

Slowly, she complied, allowing her clothing to pool at her feet. One hand on the cool, cotton and she longed to feel it caressing her skin. She smoothed the other hand over the sheet-covered table.

"Are you going to fondle the sheet or actually get on the table so I can help you?"

She slid on the table, allowing her feet to dangle. For the first time in a long time, she felt exposed. She wanted nothing more than to cross her arms over her breasts, but she did cross her legs.

"I haven't seen that look in a while."

"What look?"

He brushed her hair from her face and traced the tiny scar near her hairline. She went still. "The one that hovers between fight and flight. You're not sure if I'm going to hurt or help you." Joshua swept his fingers over her cheek, down her throat, and along her shoulder. "I'm here to help and give you what you need. Now lay on your stomach and relax."

She complied and something warm was placed over her limbs.

"Are you comfortable?" Instrumental jazz wafted through the air at a barely discernible level. "Or do you prefer the sound of water?" His voice was gentle and soothing.

"The music is fine." She adjusted her face on the pillow but couldn't find the right spot. A couple of clicks raised the headrest where it needed to be.

"Better?"

"Thank you."

"Just lie there a moment," he said. "I'm going to fill a bowl of water for Kiska and be right back."

She listened as his footsteps faded. The splash of water as it hit a container, then stopped as his footsteps returned. She twisted her head in time to see a splash of bright blue.

It was one of the few colors she could still see. One of the things she enjoyed doing was staring at the sky on a clear day. She could feel the heat of the sun but would never see its brilliance. She didn't need to see a raindrop to know it was wet and could be cold. The things she couldn't see, she could feel. What she couldn't touch, well...it didn't really exist for her.

The warmth of the blanket seeped into her aching body, and on an exhale, she allowed her body to sink into the satiny sheet beneath her, marveling at the way both fabrics soothed and comforted her.

"You seem more relaxed." His voice was so soft and gentle, she barely caught the sound.

"Yes, as much as I can be at the moment."

"Let's see what we can do about getting you fully relaxed."

A slight chill skittered down her spine before it was replaced by warm liquid and firm hands. An involuntary sigh brushed her lips as he worked a tough knot from her shoulders.

"You always carried a lot of tension in your neck. When was the last time these kinks wore worked out?"

"It's been a minute." She turned her head on the pillow, resting her cheek against the cushion. "The last few weeks Gareth became overprotective and really didn't let me out of his sight."

"Really?" He moved down her spine, circling each vertebrae. When he reached the curve of her buttocks, he worked his way back up. Each pass left her more relaxed, and she sank a little deeper into the cushion.

"Mmmm."

The sheet was placed over her back once more, and he removed her right arm. Starting with her fingers, he smoothed his thumbs over each digit, up her forearm, to her bicep, and back down again. Just the way she remembered.

Joshua tucked her arm beneath the blanket again, reached beneath the covering, and kneaded her shoulders. Amelia wasn't as rigid as before, her muscles looser. A small wave of satisfaction washed through him, followed by a hot wave of desire. He wanted to do more than just massage Amelia's aches and pains away, but that's what she needed right now. He wanted a repeat of this morning, but that would have to wait.

He glanced over his shoulder and found the dog lapping her water. Kiska was fine, and he returned his attention to Amelia. He grabbed a small bottle of oil and poured more into his palm. "What about visitors?"

This line of questioning probably wasn't conducive to a soothing environment, but one thing he knew about his Lia, as long as he kept her calm, she'd tell him everything he needed to know.

"Only those we both trusted, and that wasn't a very long list. I used to tease him about his paranoia. He used to tell me, he'd gladly be paranoid as long as it kept me safe. I was too important to entrust to just anyone. He even restricted my family from visiting."

"I would ban your family from being anywhere near you. They are toxic and never had your best interests at heart."

She chuckled. "I think part of that is my grandmother's doing. She wanted to make sure I received the care I needed for the rest of my life. She didn't trust my parents to do it."

"I remember your grandmother. She was a very savvy woman."

"She really liked you."

They fell silent as he worked the kinks and soreness from her limbs.

After a while, he said, "I was there for her funeral."

She tensed beneath his hands, and he ran his fingers over her calve muscles. "You were there?" Her voice broke. "Why didn't you say something?"

He blew out a breath. "I couldn't even get near you, Lia. Hell, I wasn't even supposed to be at the funeral, but I couldn't *not* pay my respects. She fought for me. For us."

"She did. Even when I married Gareth, she didn't like that I didn't mourn you long enough, but she understood. Probably more than I did at that time. I lost her six months after you." A catch was in her voice. "I almost didn't make it through that year." She sighed. "I wanted the comfort of your arms so bad. Even now, but I'll settle for the massage."

Joshua leaned close, skimming his lips along the shell of her ear. "You've never had to settle for anything. I'm here and will comfort you as much as you need."

She shrugged off his hands. "You don't want me, Joshua. You're only here to protect me. You want to punish me for divorcing you, but I can't make up for those years. No matter how hard I try, I can't erase what's been done to us." Her voice broke.

He lowered his head as his heart clenched. That's all he'd been doing was giving her a hard time. Not once had he stopped to consider how all of this had affected her. He'd been so caught up in the abandonment and the payout. Before he could question his motives, he rolled

Amelia in the blanket, gathered her close, and carried her to a nearby sofa.

"Hey! What are you doing?" She kicked her legs and shoved at his shoulders.

"Be still. I don't want to drop you." For added measure, he swatted her behind. She stilled in his arms. He sat with her in his lap and held her close. "You need comfort. That I can provide."

"Don't play with my emotions, Joshua. I can't handle this right now."

"Would you prefer I take you over my knee and redden that pretty bottom until you cry?" The way her lips parted into an 'o' and went rigid in his arms almost had him chuckling. There was no denying the flare of desire in her irises. She'd derive as much pleasure from the experience as she would relief. He smoothed her hair from her forehead. "But this is what you want." He wrapped his arms around her. "I know it is."

For several heartbeats, she remained stiff in his embrace. The play of emotions on her face was astounding. Fear skittered into doubt before acceptance finally won. She relaxed against him, and he drew her closer.

Lia buried her face in the hollow of his shoulder, then her body began to shake in his arms. Dampness wet his skin, and he held her tighter. "I'm here, and I'm not going anywhere." He kept his voice soothing and gentle.

"You can't make that promise."

He opened his mouth to protest, then slowly closed it. She was right. He really couldn't make that promise. Anything could happen, but as long as he was here... "You're right. I won't promise you that. However, I will protect you with my life and find out who ripped us apart. I will make them pay."

They sat there a long time. Joshua would sit for an eternity if it meant keeping her in his arms. "I never stopped loving you, Lia."

Joshua carried Amelia to bed. Her deep, even breathing signaled she'd fallen asleep. Kiska trotted behind him. He glanced between the two rooms, then at the animal.

"I'm watching guard over her. Is that all right with you?" He deposited her in the middle of the king-size bed.

Her lids briefly fluttered before they opened. "Massage over already?"

He swept a caress over the curve of her cheek. "Yes. This is the second part of your relaxation program."

"You're such a bully."

He chuckled. "Think what you like, but we've got three years to make up for."

"We can't get those years back."

"No, we can't." He quickly shed his clothes and slid underneath the covers beside her. He gathered her close, resting his chin on her head as she settled into his arms. "You are safe, Amelia. I won't let anyone hurt you."

She nodded, her hair tangling in his beard. "I'm glad." A moment later, she was sound asleep.

Joshua laid there a long time, just holding her. A luxury he missed most of all. Everything he'd seen and learned over the past few days about Amelia couldn't compare to what he wanted to know. One thing was certain, someone in her family wanted her out of the way, so they could have unencumbered access to her money.

At this point, he was certain that was why Gareth was killed. Maybe he would visit the scene of the crime and see if there was anything he could find.

Chapter Eleven

"Can I help you with something?"

Joshua turned at the newcomer's sarcastic tone. The social secretary stood with his back to the sun. Joshua still couldn't remember the man's name. He shifted, just a hair, and Joshua noticed a few fresh bruises just above the collar of his starched white shirt.

The man stepped to his right and once more he was shadowed.

"Who let you on the premises?" Joshua asked.

The man colored. "I'm here to collect my belongings. Your guard dog is over there." He indicated to a beefy-looking man about twenty yards away. The guard lifted a hand as two men in t-shirts, with the name of a moving company emblazoned across the chest, carried boxes.

"I see."

"You don't belong here," the man sneered.

"And which one of us is moving?" he responded pleasantly.

"You some kind of freak who likes looking at crime scenes?"

"Not really. Amelia mentioned Gareth died in his studio." He turned back toward the structure but kept an eye on the other.

"I'm surprised she remembered."

"I doubt Amelia forgets much of anything once she's been told," Joshua said. The man moved again, and this time, fresh scratches were visible on the backs of his hand. Curious. "Have you been doing some gardening?"

"I'm sorry?"

"You should really wear gloves if you're going to work with the roses," Joshua continued, as if he hadn't spoken. "Sometimes those scratches can get infected. I hear the cure can be very painful." The sun moved behind a cloud just enough to eliminate the shadow on the man's face; Joshua read fear and anger before it slid behind a mask of civility.

"I'll take that under advisement." He offered a nervous chuckle. "What else does Amelia remember?"

Joshua studied the charred remains of the building in front of him. He moved forward, aware of the other man's scrutiny. Something about the blast radius and the other marks bothered him. He stepped to the yellow caution tape and pushed it aside.

"You really shouldn't do that. The authorities haven't cleared the building for anyone to go in."

"It's okay. I know a thing or two about burnt buildings and such."

"Why does this even matter to you? You're not even her husband anymore." Impatience and anger filled the other man's tone.

"Yes. There is that little detail. Along with the fact that someone murdered my best friend." Joshua hardened his voice. "You wouldn't happen to know anything about that or who could be stealing Amelia's money?"

A flicker of doubt crossed the man's face. Joshua was definitely on the right track, and the social secretary knew more than what he was telling. Had Gareth found something that pointed to this man? Maybe that's what got him killed.

"Perhaps Gareth asked one too many questions to the wrong person. Not everyone likes being interrogated."

Joshua focused squarely on the taller man. "Do you feel as if you're being interrogated?" He missed nothing of the man's expression. Not the slight downward twist of his lips or the faint crinkling of his eyes. "I believe you're the one with something to hide. You keep track of everything the family does, where they're supposed to be, and who they're supposed to see."

"The family values my services." He pulled at his cuffs. "Or at least, they did until Gage terminated my employment."

"Indeed. So how is Victor?" Joshua scrutinized the other's face for any sign of deception. "I hear he had a bad accident and is now in the hospital."

He flinched, then tried to roll his shoulders. "He and Gareth were very close. That's no secret. I believe the fellow was distraught enough to take his own life and tried."

Joshua nodded. Once he learned of Victor's condition, he posted a guard on the man. If someone did try to finish him off, at least this way, it would be more difficult. Once Victor awakened, Joshua would question him about what happened. He half turned. "Don't let me keep you from coordinating your move. I know how that must keep you busy."

The other stood stiffly for a moment, then spun on his heel and marched away. Joshua followed his progress until he disappeared around a bend in the path. He would have to keep an eye on that man and dig a little deeper into the information he already had.

He returned his attention to the building and carefully picked his way through the structure. The scent of charred, wet wood and chemicals, though faint, still clung to the air. Broken glass crunched beneath his boot as he methodically walked the room.

Photos, their frames twisted and warped from the heat, stared at him from the only wall untouched by the blast. Joshua paused at a picture of him and Amelia. Despite the smoke and water damage to the paper, it was still provocative. Amelia wore a corset, her breasts barely contained in the dark material as she kneeled before him. He'd grabbed a fistful of her hair. He could still remember her sigh as her lips had parted while she gazed up at him. Her eyes were unfocused, but the adoration and trust were visible.

His other hand held her throat, a flash of metal rested on one knuckle. Gareth had captured the moment he collared Amelia perfectly, that moment where she had pledged her submission to Joshua as he vowed to give her his protection for all time. A promise so intimate, he valued it as the rare and precious gift it was.

Joshua drew a ragged breath and swallowed the emotion coating his throat. *I will find out who did this.*

Amelia couldn't move. She dragged a shuttered breath into her lungs. Why was it so hot in here? "Gareth? We should stop. Something's not right."

Silence.

"Gareth?" A dull sense of panic gripped her. He wouldn't just leave her like this, would he? She fumbled with the brake. Her movements sluggish and clumsy. It took her three tries to anchor the rope so she wouldn't fall. She briefly hung, fingers grazing the soft nap of the carpet. It was just enough to prevent her from spinning, yet the sensation persisted. She pressed her palm harder into the floor. The spinning did not stop.

"Gareth! Something's wrong. Pickles!" She fumbled for her bra strap, searching for the safety scissors tied there.

They weren't there.

She pawed at each strap. Her fingers wouldn't cooperate. Touching the cool blades calmed her some, but now, she couldn't get the scissors to the rope.

"Pickles, Gareth. Pickles."

Silence.

Why didn't he answer her? And where was Victor? He should've been spotting too. For the first time in a long time, she felt vulnerable and exposed. "Gar—"

"Shhh."

She turned her head in the direction of the male voice. Not Gareth. "Who's there? Where's Gareth?"

Rough fingers grazed her bare back. She recoiled from the touch. "Don't."

"I've waited a long time for this," he continued, as if she hadn't spoken. "Will you scream for me?"

Before she could comprehend his meaning, the first stinging stripe of a single tail whip flayed her naked flesh.

Breath left her body as the second and third strikes fell. She didn't remember screaming, only crying and laughter. His horrible glee at her humiliation.

Hands gripped her wrists, and she fought against the hold.

"Amelia. Stop! Stop. You're dreaming."

The voice. The voice was so familiar and yet...

"C'mon, Lia. Stop fighting me. I'm not going to hurt you."

His touch was firm but gentle, his voice commanding yet soothing. She stilled her efforts but fought to get breath into her lungs. She was breathing way too fast. She pushed against the solid wall of muscle beneath her cheek.

"I can't." She gasped. How did she tell him she couldn't get her breathing under control, that she couldn't focus enough to grab a decent breath?

"I know, baby. Just breathe with me." Gentle hands cupped her face before clearing her tears. He placed one hand on his chest and left the other on her cheek. "In and out, Lia. In and out."

She struggled to follow his deep, slow breaths.

"You can do this. We can do this together. You're safe with me. Always safe with me," he said.

Amelia blinked back more hot tears. She had been and was safe with him. Even now, security wrapped around her, holding her close in its warm embrace. With effort, she focused on the way his chest moved beneath her hand and followed the movement.

One breath. Two. By the third, tension seeped from her limbs.

"Keep going, love. You're doing good."

Encouraged, she continued following his lead. In and out. The rise and fall of his chest comforting beneath her palm. In. Up. Out. Down. Safe. Each breath she took hammered that fact home. Safe. *I am safe.*

She leaned against his chest, settling her ear over his heart. "I couldn't move."

"Hmm?"

"I couldn't move. My hands wouldn't work right, and I couldn't get the scissors to cut the rope."

"Who bound you?"

She smiled. "I self-tied, doing suspension. He was there, laughing at my humiliation, at my vulnerability. He laughed and kept whipping me until he stopped."

"What made him stop?" Joshua asked quietly.

What made him stop? Amelia pulled away, drew her knees to her chest, wrapped her arms around her shins, and rested her chin on her knees. Something. Something made him stop. A noise of some sort that she'd never heard before and hadn't heard since.

"A sound. A tone or something," she answered.

"Can you remember what it sounded like?"

She shook her head. "No. I just thought it odd. I need to lay down." Amelia settled beneath the covers, grateful when Joshua wrapped his body around hers. She inhaled. A faint trace of smoke and burnt wood lingered on his skin. "Where have you been?"

"Investigating where Gareth died."

"Oh."

"Funny thing. I ran into that social secretary clown."

"Dawson Cahill?"

"That's his name? No wonder I couldn't remember it."

She chuckled. "I don't like him either. I never have."

"Then it's a good thing Gage fired him. If you didn't like him, why was he here?"

"Gareth's parents hired him to coordinate appearances." Amelia pillowed her head on his chest, settling more fully into his embrace. "Kiska doesn't like him either."

"Something's not right about him. He seems to know more than he lets on."

"What do you mean?"

"He didn't want me looking around Gareth's studio, and I think he may have something to do with Victor being in the hospital."

Amelia sat straight up. "Victor is in the hospital? Ohmygosh. Why didn't you say something?" She swung her legs off the bed. With one hand out, she felt her way toward the door. "What happened?"

"Lia? Where are you going?" Bed springs creaked as he shifted his weight.

"I need to see him. Gareth would never forgive me if I didn't at least visit and make sure he was all right."

"He wouldn't know you were there."

She skidded to a halt. "I get the impression you don't want me to visit him."

He stood behind her. "Someone tried to kill him. Probably the same person trying to kill you."

"A-are you sure?"

"I'm not so sure he wasn't involved in what happened to you or what happened to Gareth."

Her eyebrows climbed her forehead. "You think Victor was involved? No. I can't believe that. He loved Gareth more than anything. He would never do anything to hurt him."

"What about you?" Joshua whispered against her cheek. "You had everything Victor wanted. You had his name. His money and even a lot of his attention. I'm willing to bet you shared many of his nights too."

She covered her ears. "Stop it. Stop it! Victor wouldn't violate my trust like that."

"Jealousy changes people, Lia." He caressed her arm. "I'm not trying to hurt you with this, but you had everything Victor ever wanted. The open accolades as his spouse, the acceptance." He led her back to the bed and forced her to sit.

"Our marriage was in name only. I knew that. Victor knew that. Gareth was there to protect me, and I protected his and Victor's relationship. Without me, they wouldn't have had the freedom they had."

"Maybe he didn't see it like that."

"They lived together." She shook her head. "I can't believe he would let someone walk in and just hurt me like that."

"I have an appointment to check out the tapes at the club tonight."

"Then we'll go there. After that, take me to see Victor."

"Lia."

"If he's the one that let someone hurt me, I want to see him."

Later that evening, Joshua paused at the threshold of the fetish club—where he first played with Amelia. She was uncollared and was just someone he had to get to know better. They came here often, and now he had to find out who hurt her.

He shook the ghosts from his shoulders, patted Amelia's hand, and led them up the steep flight of stairs. Kiska followed close behind.

"Sir J." A tall lanky man greeted with genuine warmth. "It's so good to see you again."

"Dennis. Likewise." Joshua shook his hand. "Is everything set up?"

"Once Two-Z told me what you were asking, I'll admit we don't normally keep anything that far back, but because of the circumstances, that night's tapes are the only ones we kept."

Joshua nodded. "Did you view what happened?" They walked around a scarred wooden waist-high counter, through an entryway into back hall. He leaned toward Amelia. "We're headed to the security office."

She nodded. The tight grip on his arm was the only indication of any type of agitation.

"We all heard of your death," Dennis began. "I'm glad the folks got it wrong this time." He tossed a grin over his shoulder. "You weren't marooned on some island and trained as a ninja, then comeback as a vigilante ready to take down the corrupt leaders of the city, are you?"

Joshua chuckled. "No. Just doing my best to reclaim life and make a new future."

Dennis nodded and opened the office door. "I set everything up. Holler if you need anything." He stepped back and allowed them into the room, then closed the door.

Joshua led Amelia to a chair and set her hand on the back of it. He waited until she settled in the chair before he sat in the one next to hers and rolled closer to the black, metal desk.

In front of him were several monitors, each showing a different angle or room of the club. On the large screen before him was a still image of three people. Inhaling a deep breath, he pressed play.

"Joshua? Is everything okay?" Concern filled Amelia's voice. "Your breathing changed. Is there something bad on the tape?"

"No, sweetheart. I'm concerned about what I'm about to see." He would have to remember to control his reactions better. He reached over and patted her hand. "Just give me a moment to look through everything."

He tapped a couple of keys, and the action sped up ten times. Instead of a grainy image, high-definition clear pixels dominated the screen. There was Amelia as she said, nude and strapped to the spanking bench. Several welts adorned her ample derriere, courtesy of the pinky thick cane in Gareth's hand. Every now and then, he would pause to caress her buttocks. At one point, he seemed to stumble, and Joshua rewound the tape to see it again. He let it play forward. He checked the time. Just ten minutes in play.

They moved from the bench. Victor stepped into the frame laying out coils of rope in various colors.

The men erected a self-standing suspension rig while Amelia worked the ropes into a harness around her ankles, thighs, and hips.

Gareth stepped to her, checking the knots. She gave him a gentle shove. He smiled and walked away leaving her to rig the ropes into a diamond shape with five openings.

Gareth and Victor settled long one wall, watching Amelia rise and spin.

Another pause. This time for water. Gareth made sure Amelia drank nearly half the bottle before he finished off the rest. A sense of approval washed over him. Gareth really did take care of his Amelia. From making sure she was hydrated to keeping constant contact with her. Not once had he stopped touching her.

Tension crept through his body. Her movements weren't as sure now. Amelia's movements weren't as smooth. Several times the rope seemed to slide through her fingers before she could tighten her grip.

Joshua didn't need sound to understand she was asking to stop.

Movement from the lower corner of the screen caught his eye. For the first time, Victor moved. Joshua had nearly forgotten he was there until then. Fascinated, he watched as Victor stood, seeming to wait. Once Gareth fell to the floor, the other man walked past. Not in a hurry nor did he stop to check that his partner was okay. He crossed straight to the door and opened it.

"Joshua?"

"Not now, Lia." His tone was harsher than he intended, but Victor helped hurt Amelia and that was unacceptable. Once Victor woke up, he would answer for his role. Now Joshua needed to see who walked in the room.

The face was masked, and he wore a leather collar that read Pet, but he recognized the man's build striding into the room with a single tail whip. The same man who'd glared at Amelia during her police interview. Victor quickly closed the door. The man's lips moved as he approached Amelia.

She flinched at his touch and shook her head. Clearly, her lips forming the word, 'pickles.' When the first strike fell, he couldn't stop his body from jerking in response. Kiska whined behind him.

Fury, so hot, it flowed through his veins, engulfing him. He balled his hands into fists. It wasn't until Amelia jerked on his pant leg that he realized he was standing.

"You know who did this to me. To us?"

He didn't dare touch her. He didn't think he could keep his emotions from spilling over into his touch. Instead, he stepped away from her. "I do. And unfortunately, Victor was involved."

Chapter Twelve

Amelia stood next to the hospital bed. One hand gripped the railing while the other held the fingers of the man she thought was her friend. She wished she could see more than the blurred shadow of a shapeless blob.

"I still can't believe you were involved, Victor." Amelia squeezed his hand. "And look at you now. Someone tried to kill you too? Was it worth it? Was it worth Gareth's life or even mine?"

The blips of the heart monitor and the steady drip of the IV were her answer.

"I wish you could tell me why you did this. Why you felt you had to take Gareth away from both of us, and why you felt like you had to take Joshua away from me in the first place?"

The squeak of rubber soles grabbed her attention, and she reached for the harness on Kiska's back. At the low growl, Amelia froze. "What is it? Joshua?" she called out, then to her dog, "To the door." She followed the dog around the bed and to the door where both animal and woman stopped.

The scent of sweat and old leather mingled with a faint hint of garlic caused her stomach to roll. Amelia stumbled back with a gasp. Kiska barked, as if sensing her agitation.

"Who's there?" Amelia couldn't keep the wobble from her voice. "Joshua."

Cold fingers closed around her wrist. She screamed, pulled her arm back for a solar plexus punch and let the blow fly. A soft whoosh of breath leaving a body greeted her ears.

"Let's go, Kiska." The dog brushed her knees. Amelia twined her fingers into the animal's fur and allowed her to propel her forward. Footsteps pounded behind them. "The elevator, girl."

Where is Joshua? That thought was uppermost in Amelia's mind as she hurried forward. *He is right.* She shouldn't have come to the hospital. *Oh gosh. Where am I?* Amelia patted the wall in front of her for what she hoped were the elevator buttons. She didn't care if the car was going up or down as long as it took her away from the man trying to grab her.

Strong hands grabbed her shoulders, and she let out a squeak.

"Amelia! Where the hell are you running to."

She clutched the front of Joshua's shirt and buried her nose into the cloth. Earthy musk greeted her. He wrapped an arm around her waist and drew her closer.

"He-he was here. He was in the room with me and Victor. I didn't know where you were or anything. I had to get out of there."

Joshua gently lifted her chin until the breath from his exhale hit her cheeks. "Slow down, honey. Who was in the room?"

"The man who hurt me. He was there."

"Calm down, Lia. No one was in the room but Victor. I saw you running down the hall."

She shook her head. "I punched him in the solar plexus. He was there, Joshua."

"I'm not doubting you. I'm just saying no one was in the room when I looked."

"I thought you had someone watching the room. Why wasn't he there?"

He cupped her face. "Come on, Lia, breathe with me. You're getting worked up." His voice was calm and soothing. "Just in and out, baby. You're safe."

She gripped his wrists and breathed in and out. As long as he was touching her, she was safe. No one could harm her.

"Please believe me, Joshua." Amelia couldn't keep the plea from her voice.

"I do." Truth rang in his words. "I'm going to lead you to a consultation room where my colleague, Dakota Mills, is at. We call him Kota. He will sit with you until I return."

"No, I don't..."

"I know you don't want me to leave you alone, but you won't rest until I discover who tried to grabbed you," he said as they continued to walk.

A sweeter scent, almost like almonds, mingled with cool masculinity greeted her nostrils.

"Amelia, this is Kota."

"I've heard a lot about you, Amelia."

A gentle but firm hand gripped her elbow. She couldn't stop the flinch that rushed through her body. Immediately, the hand fell away.

"Oh. I'm so sorry. I forgot about you not liking to be touched by strangers. Trust that Joshua is already glaring at me," Kota said.

Despite her reservations, Amelia giggled. "I'm sure he is."

"Be very careful with her." A note of warning clung to Joshua's tone. "She means the world to me."

"I will treat her as if she's my own," Kota vowed. "If you will allow me to lead you inside, I would appreciate it."

Amelia nodded and held out her hand. Firm fingers. Familiar fingers grasped hers and placed them on a rough sleeve. Warm spice enveloped her senses as a bristly cheek brushed against hers.

"I will be back to get you. I promise...you'll be safe with Kota." With that, Joshua was gone.

"He really does worry about you." Kota placed her hand on the back of a chair.

Amelia trailed her fingers along the coarse fabric until she found the seat, then sat down. Kiska nudged her knees before laying at Amelia's feet.

"If you don't mind my asking, how did you lose your sight?"

Joshua closed the door behind him, then first looked left, then right. He'd caught a glimpse of the man who'd tried to pull Amelia away, but he had not reached either of them in time. What he hadn't told Amelia was the man had managed to jump out the window.

The fact that he escaped wasn't an issue. Joshua knew exactly who he was looking for now. All he had to do was make sure Victor wasn't killed by his accomplice. So far so good. Victor would make a full recovery, if he could just find the will to live, and Joshua didn't think Victor had enough of that left in him. Not after losing Gareth and living with the knowledge that he was responsible for that. No. Joshua didn't believe Victor could face the ugly truth of his actions.

No matter what he did, Joshua had a job to do, and that was to keep Amelia alive. He rounded the corner and the sound of the ICU blips and beeps greeted his ears. A few nurses in scrubs milled around. He slipped into Victor's room.

Joshua crossed to the bed and leaned close to the man lying there. "Listen to me, you miserable piece of shit. You're in this bed because you were stupid and greedy and weak. You got your lover killed because of that same weakness. And you tried to destroy me and Amelia because of that same weakness." Joshua breathed deep, grappling with his temper. It would be too easy, way too easy to end this man's pathetic existence. "I will find your secret, and I will make sure your accomplices are punished."

Before he could give in to his need to throttle Victor, Joshua left. There was one more man he needed to visit.

Joshua sat in the passenger seat of Kota's Jeep and stared up at the five-story brick building. Next to it was a boutique hotel owned by a local family. A uniformed doorman stood at attention on the sidewalk in front of the entryway. Joshua returned his attention to the brick building.

"Are you sure you want to do this?" Kota asked, drumming his fingers on the steering wheel.

"He stood there, glaring at her, pretending as though he had every right to be inside her home." Joshua placed his hand on the door handle. "He hurt Amelia when she was at her most vulnerable. I can't forgive that." He stepped out the vehicle. "He needs to understand there are consequences for his actions.

He slammed the car door, crossed the expanse of sidewalk, then mounted the wide, steep steps that led him to the second-floor reception area of the dungeon/sex club. The muted, pulsing of a deep bass line thrummed through the foyer. A skinny black man with a black tee shirt with staff emblazoned across the chest flicked him nod in greeting.

"What room?" Joshua demanded.

The skinny man tapped a couple of keys. "Room 3B. Fourth floor."

Joshua nodded. He walked into a small alcove where a set of elevators waited. He entered a car, and a moment later, it dumped him on the fourth floor. More music spilled out. Grunts and groans swelled with the beat. Warm bodies, in an array of undress, glided in and out of the various rooms.

More staff in dark tees kept an eye on the adults at play. The club had strict rules governing behavior and privacy. Tonight…he was going to break one of those rules to exact his revenge.

Joshua didn't acknowledge the men and women whispering his name or wished him a greeting. He kept his focus on 3B, a room halfway down the hall, one of the few rooms with a door. There were observation booths on either side, and Joshua had been assured those rooms were clear for this purpose.

He walked into the room. A woman in a leather bustier, fishnet stockings, and stilettos wielded a single tail whip with confidence and expertise.

He briefly watched as she switched between the whip and a flogger with leather tails. The man's back was a crisscross of angry, red welts.

The man, clad in a leather face mask, was bound between two posts. Joshua eyed the restraints, at the padded cuffs at his wrists. His legs were unfettered, but his feet were bare beneath his cotton trousers.

Satisfied with the setup, Joshua moved farther into the room.

Wordlessly, Two-Z handed him the whip.

"Are we done, Mistress?" the man asked.

The door closed with a decisive click.

"Not at all, Chad." Joshua flicked the whip near Chad's right hip.

Chad stiffened, flinching away from the crack. "You're not supposed to be here." He tugged on the restraints.

Joshua cracked the whip again. And again, Chad flinched away.

"What's the matter, Chad? Is it not the pleasure you had envisioned?" This time he shifted, allowing the tip to kiss the man's flesh. Skin parted and blood trickled out.

Chad hissed. "You can't do this to me!"

Crack. More blood.

"Stop this."

Snap! Snap! More blood. This time he solicited a whimper from Chad.

"Do you know who I am?" Pain dripped from the man's voice as easily as the red staining his back.

Joshua lowered the whip and approached the man. He worked the laces, then removed the mask. He tossed it aside. "I know exactly who you are." He stared straight into Chad's eyes. Fear and quiet resignation filled this man's irises.

Chad licked his lips. "Don't do this," he pleaded, agony creasing his soft features.

In that instant, Joshua knew this man unaccustomed to pain from what a true sadist could bring him. Chad played at it, skirting the very edges of when pain shifts into pleasure, but he more enjoyed hurting others—hurting Amelia. Not because she would gain anything, but because he could break her. Because he relished hurting anyone he deemed vulnerable. What it boiled down to…Chad was a bully, and Joshua knew how to deal with bullies. "Is that what Amelia said to you that night?" Joshua tossed the whip aside, then unbuckled the restraints.

Warily, Chad backed away, rubbing his wrists. "You're letting me go?" His tone was incredulous.

Joshua moved to stand in front of the door. He offered the man a mirthless smile. "Sure. If you think you're man enough to go through me."

Chad balled his hands into fists and rushed Joshua.

Joshua pivoted, slamming a left cross in Chad's soft chin, then another into his flabby belly. When Chad doubled, Joshua jabbed his knee into his face. The man dropped to the floor barely conscious.

Joshua crouched over him. "It took a moment, but I remembered you. You delivered the divorce papers and check. I won't kill you, but you will spend significant time in a cage. I hope Big Bubba makes you his bitch." Joshua walked from the room and never looked back.

Chapter Thirteen

"You said he wouldn't come back," Leigh raged. "You said you had a foolproof plan to get the portion of Hester Lee's estate back to my family. You said you had this under control!"

"How was I supposed to know Gareth was going to find Joshua," Dawson spat.

"You were hired to keep tabs on the household."

"And I did that! Who told you Victor had a fling with Gareth's parents, and she got pregnant? Who told you Gage's paternity is in question? Who told you Victor was gambling again? I did that! All I've gotten out of this is getting fired by some fagot's offspring."

"Did you at least eliminate Victor?" One look at his face and she knew the truth. "You are totally worthless." She reached for another bottle of alcohol. "All the men in my life are worthless. Even Chad couldn't accomplish the task I gave him. He managed to get fired too."

"He can't talk right now. Can you have your contact transfer his funds? Passwords and account numbers have been changed on my end."

Her smile was thin. "There have been some transition and reorganizing as you can imagine at the firm." She crossed the room, peruse the selections on the hotel mini bar, before retrieving a small bottle of whiskey. She didn't bother with a glass. "Perhaps you should have made sure you had those items in hand before you killed Gareth."

"He was getting too close."

"There are still too many loose ends."

"If I try for Amelia now..." He let the sentence hang.

"What about Gage?"

"Victor, if he lives, inherits." Dawson watched her down the whiskey. "As it is, getting near either one will be twice as hard. The estate is crawling with security. I tried to smuggle out a few items and was caught. I tried to leave behind a few electronic eyes, and they were confiscated. They were interviewing the staff. We have been successfully locked out."

She drained the bottle, then threw it into the trash. "If we can't take out either of them, we take out Joshua." With him out of the way, we can drain her dry.

The law firm was empty and quiet, except for the hum of electronics. Not even the click-clack of keys from a paralegal or associate was heard.

Amelia sat behind Gareth's desk, sifting through files. A lump rose in her throat as his peppery masculinity surrounded her. He'd been a very good friend. Her fingers trembled as they skimmed over the braille.

He made sure all of his files were in braille so she would have access. She was glad for that small bit of foresight.

There had to be a reason for Gareth's secrecy. With is studio destroyed, something had to be here in his office. She stood, circled the desk, and went to the file cabinet. The drawer slid open on noiseless rails. She thumbed through the tabs, only stopping when she came to a file with her name. Frowning, she extracted the file, slightly surprised at the heft. Using the surface of the cabinet as a desk, she carefully opened the file.

Not all the documents were in braille. She'd have to grab a scanner to read the document for her. What she did find in braille was enough to anger and fill her with infinite sadness.

"Did you find anything?" Joshua asked as he entered the office.

She nodded. "I did." She held out a sheaf of papers, the ones she couldn't read. "She's been stealing from the trusts." Even to her ears, her voice was weary. "Pretending you were dead, trying to kill me, and killing Gareth were all a cover up while she stole from the trusts."

"Who?" The faint scent of oranges wafted through the air, followed by the rustle of fabric. Joshua grunted as he grasped her. They both fell to the floor.

Warmth trickled down her face; and her ears rang. Joshua lay still and heavy on top of her.

"Joshua," she murmured.

"I really wish you hadn't found that information," Leigh told her. "If that damn dog hadn't dragged you out the road that night, none of this would've happened."

Amelia didn't hear her; she was too focused on Joshua. He was too still. "Joshua?" She brushed her hand over him, recoiling when one came away wet. "No. No. No." He couldn't be dead. Not when she just learned he was alive again. "Please, Joshua. Don't leave me. Please don't leave me."

"Get up, Amelia."

Amelia stayed where she was, stroking Joshua's hair as she cradled him in her lap. "Go away, Leigh."

"I will put another bullet in your precious Joshua if you don't do exactly what I say."

Amelia laid a palm on Joshua's chest. Relief flooded her limbs and made her giddy at the strong beat beneath her hand. He was alive. Now, she had to keep him that way.

She gently laid his head on the floor, then slowly gained her feet. She felt around, trying to determine where they had fallen in the room. Her searching fingers met the gritty wheel of the executive chair. Okay. They'd fallen behind the desk. She could use that.

Using the desk as a guide, she followed it around until the scent of oranges and cordite strengthened. "You've planned this a very long time."

"And my plan would've worked perfectly, if Hester Lee hadn't changed her will."

Realization dawned, and Amelia stumbled, almost falling if the desk wasn't at her back. "You killed her."

Amelia couldn't see the smile, but it was definitely in Leigh's voice. "She confronted me about some checks and suspicious transfers from her accounts and yours."

A rustle of fabric gave Amelia the impression the woman was shrugging.

"She threatened to go to the authorities. I couldn't have that."

"So you killed her," Amelia whispered.

"After I managed to get rid of Joshua, Chad was very helpful at drawing up the paperwork and delivering what

I needed. All he had to do was stay dead to you. That was another reason Hester had to go. She knew Joshua wasn't dead, and she was going to tell you."

Amelia leaned against the desk. *I can't believe anyone can hold so much hate and loathing in their heart. All for money.* "You had your own inheritance."

"I wasn't as savvy with my funds. Too trusting with the men who said they loved me." Bitterness infused every syllable. "And you who aren't even her blood kin receive the bulk of her estate. And before that, you have an absolutely gorgeous man madly in love with you. You can't even see him! And he loves you. A helpless blind woman."

"Leigh."

"How is that fair? I'm the eldest. I'm blood, but everyone bows to you like you're special."

Amelia slid a step forward. If she could keep Leigh talking, she could maybe give Joshua a chance. At least she hoped she was hearing Joshua move behind the desk.

"So you had Gareth killed."

"Yes. I bought Victor's markers. I didn't expect him to go all noble. Stupid fag."

"Down!"

Amelia hit the floor, curling into a ball as wind whipped across her. A scream, followed by a pop and a thud, kept her curled on the floor.

Muffled crying and cursing filled the silence.

The sound of material ripping and a yelp filled her ears. "Joshua?"

"She's subdued, Lia." Vibrations of footsteps reached her a moment before Joshua helped her to her feet. He brushed the hair from her face. "Are you hurt?"

"No, but you are."

He chuckled. "Just a flesh wound. A couple of stitches and I'll be fine."

She wrapped her arms around his waist as his good arm held her close. She buried her nose, inhaling his scent and wept.

Epilogue

The deep bass of a b-Flat tuba resounded off the rafter and acoustic walls to a rich mellow timbre. The song, a jaunty little number streaked with humor, showcased the player's prowess with the instrument. As the last note trailed off, a rousing applause filled the recital hall.

Amelia joined in, rising to her feet as the ovation swelled around her.

"He's wonderful," Joshua murmured into her ear.

"He is."

"Since we're standing, let's make our way out to the foyer."

While others still clapped and rummaged around, Joshua led Amelia and her guide to an alcove out of the way.

With the ensuing months sorting out the disaster Leigh wrought, nothing would bring back Gareth. Nothing would fill the hole left by his presence.

Even her firm had taken a hit. Hester Lee's, as well as Amelia's, trusts had not been the only ones affected. A handful of the other trusts had been tampered with, and Chad Tyler was responsible for those. He'd been Leigh's point man on the inside.

That was in the sheaf of papers Amelia had given Joshua. Gareth found this out and had paid for it with his life.

She threaded her hand through Joshua's arm. Through it all, he'd never left her side. She pressed her nose to his shirt sleeve, inhaling his scent. She'd never get used to him and will never take his presence for granted again.

He stroked a hand down her spine to skim the curve of her buttock. "No underwear?" he said against her cheek.

"I do believe you requested that."

His soft chuckle flowed over her like warm honey. "I did."

"You made it!" Gage exclaimed as he bounded toward them.

He clasped Joshua in a hug, before doing the same to Amelia.

"Of course." You were terrific," Amelia gushed.

"I wish Gare could've been here." He touched Amelia's forearm. "Did you hear what happened to Victor?"

She nodded. Victor, unable to live with the guilt, succumbed to his injuries and never woke up. They had no choice but to remove him from life support.

Sadness, dull and achy, washed through Amelia. She'd have preferred Victor survived so she could rage at him, demand him to tell her about his part in Gareth's death, or if his plan in tearing her away from Joshua was worth the suffering he had caused them. And for what? To keep a long ago tryst a secret? To keep Gage from knowing when he already knew his parents weren't his biological parents?

Tears stung her eyes as she thought of Gareth who'd protected her, even finding Joshua for her when everyone that he was dead. And how, if Victor had confessed everything sooner, he'd have had Gareth as his spouse and she would have her Joshua.

Now all she had to remember both of these men were bittersweet memories and urns of ashes. One day, she will learn to forgive Victor in this role, but not today.

"So are you two off on your honeymoon?" Gage's question brought Amelia from her reverie.

"She's finally allowing me to take her away for two weeks, but we had to come see you first." Joshua skimmed a hand down her bare arm.

They'd married in a very quiet, very private ceremony just the day before. Amelia ran her thumb over the new set of wedding bands. Very similar to her old, except the engagement ring had five stones while the wedding band had a channel set of diamonds. Joshua wore a similar band of diamonds.

"Are you adjusting well enough?" She cupped Gage's cheek.

The corners of his mouth moved upward beneath her hand. "Well enough. The music helps a lot," he admitted. "And I've met someone."

"Oh?"

"I'll bring her home for Thanksgiving."

"Do that."

Gage stepped away. "Later."

Joshua wrapped his arm around her waist. "Come, Lia. I have some new rope I want to try out."

Author's Note

Hello, Fans and Readers.

I just wanted to pop in and give you a quick clarification about the guide dog in this book. Kiska is a fictional creation. Any trainer of guide, seeing eye, or leader dogs will tell you the animal is trained to help the blind or visually impaired navigate a sighted world. They are trained to cross streets, move us out of the path of vehicles (yes, even the electric ones), to guide us around obstacles, and keep us from falling downstairs or off curbs. This is only a fraction of what they are trained to do. Sadly, depending on your point of view, they are not trained to protect. This has been reiterated to me on numerous occasions with these wonderful trainers at Southeastern Guide Dogs, where I received my guide over two years ago.

A caveat to that is a dog is a dog. They have a fierce love and loyalty to his or her handler. While the guide may not be trained to protect, a dog's natural instinct is to protect their pack. I've witnessed this when my guide has placed himself between me and other dogs or people. Fortunately, most people I encounter are more afraid of my fur ball than he is of them. The mere sight of him is enough to scare people away.

I had fun giving Kiska a super protective and vocal personality. Hopefully, you'll love her as much as I do.

4 Horsemen Publications

Romance

Ann Shepphird
The War Council

Emily Bunney
All or Nothing
All the Way
All Night Long
All She Needs
Having it All
All at Once
All Together
All for Her

Lynn Chantale
The Baker's Touch
Blind Secrets
Broken Lens

Mimi Francis
Private Lives
Private Protection
Run Away Home
The Professor

4HorsemenPublications.com

www.ingramcontent.com/pod-product-compliance
Lightning Source LLC
LaVergne TN
LVHW041636060526
838200LV00040B/1593